Three Faces
of Love

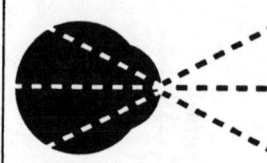

Three Faces of Love

Peggy Gaddis

Thorndike Press • Thorndike, Maine

© Copyright, 1955, by Arcadia House

All rights reserved.

Published in 1994 by arrangement with
Donald MacCampbell, Inc.

Thorndike Large Print ® Romance Series.

The tree indicium is a trademark of Thorndike Press.

The text of this Large Print edition is unabridged.
Other aspects of the book may vary from the original edition.

Set in 16 pt. News Plantin.

Printed in the United States on acid-free, high opacity paper. ∞

Library of Congress Cataloging in Publication Data

Gaddis, Peggy.
   Three faces of love / Peggy Gaddis.
     p.   cm.
   ISBN 0-7862-0151-7 (alk. paper : lg. print)
   1. Large type books. I. Title.
[PS3513.A227T48   1994]
813'.52—dc20
                                                                       93-40512

For
Sherman —
and the red roses.

Chapter 1

Lessie Howell slipped the crisply starched, faded blue gingham dress over her head, zipped it up and shook her shining blue-black hair loose about her shoulders. She brushed it vigorously, and then whipped it into a smooth gleaming knot at the back of her proudly poised head.

There had been a time when she had yearned for a permanent wave, and her hair cut into crisp, short curls. But that was a time that now seemed very long ago. A time before Dad, plowing one of the steeply sloping fields on the mountain farm, had been caught beneath the overturned tractor and killed. A time before Mom, trying frantically with her feeble strength to extricate him, had injured herself so severely that she had died less than a month later, and Lessie had had to come home and take care of the younger children.

She rarely allowed herself time to remember the days when she had stayed at Laceyville, the county seat, where she had lived with Aunt Maggie while she went to high school, seeking the education her mother had so desperately wanted all her children to have. Lessie had given up her hope of graduating with her class in June and had come home soon after Thanksgiving, to look after and bring up the five young children in the old mountain farmhouse that was more than a hundred years old. The years since then had not seemed long, for the days were too crowded for anything but hard work and the loving care of her little brood.

The morning was young and fresh as she came down the stairs toward the kitchen. It was not yet five o'clock, but the May morning was crisp and chilly.

After breakfast preparations were well started, she moved briskly to the back door, turned the key in the lock and swung it open.

A man seated comfortably on the back steps, his pipe aglow,stood up, grinning at her.

"You people sleep late around here, don't you?" he teased her.

"Why, Ben," she gasped, color warming her face, her eyes tender. "What are you doing here at this hour of the morning?"

"Waiting for sleepy-heads like you to get up and show themselves; what else?" he demanded, tall and lean and broad of shoulder in his uniform of a forest ranger. He turned to the bench beside the well and picked up a brimming bucket of foamy milk. "And while I was waiting, I thought I might as well do the chores."

"Oh, Ben, you *are* a darling!" Lessie glowed at him.

"Well, of course I am," Ben admitted with becoming modesty. "Isn't that what I've been telling you for years? Maybe some day you'll believe me."

Lessie smiled tenderly at him.

"I've just been pretending I didn't believe it," she told him gaily. "I've known it since we were infants and you used to tote my books to school and lick the boys who pulled my pigtails."

Ben had placed the bucket on the old table beside the window, and Lessie was carefully straining the milk. He leaned against the wall, his arms folded, watching her as though he felt it a great privilege to be there and to watch her swift, unconsciously graceful movements.

"I'll let you in on a little secret," he confided. "They were such lovely, fat pigtails I used to envy the boys who pulled them."

Lessie laughed at him over her shoulder.

"I don't believe a word of that; you were

much too gentle." She was tying clean white cheesecloth covers over the two big brown crocks into which she had strained the milk, and now Ben lifted them and carried them into the shed-room where it was cool and shady.

"You've been up working and you must be worn out," Lessie said after he came back. "Sit down and have some coffee while I get some breakfast ready."

"Guess I might even learn to get used to working all night if it meant always having breakfast with you like this," he said softly, and reached a hand for hers and held it against his cheek. "One of these days, Lessie — one of these days. But Lord, the waiting is tough!"

Lessie leaned above him, her cheek against his head, her free arm about him, holding him tightly. There was a darkness in her gray eyes and a droop to her pretty mouth.

"I know, darling, I know," she whispered unsteadily. "But with the kids to look after — "

"And Mother blind and Delsie needing another year before she can finish her teaching course and nobody else to keep things going — " His voice broke off, and for a moment he sat stiff and still and Lessie's heart yearned over him.

He drew her head down, kissed her warmly, and forced a very unconvincing smile.

"Oh, well, we're young." He tried very hard to make his tone light.

"I'm twenty-three, Ben." The words were forced from her against her will.

"And I'm twenty-eight," he admitted, but once more he managed an unconvincing grin. "Just a couple of aged, decrepit creatures about ready for old age assistance pension. That's us."

Because his mood was so heavy, like her own, and because he was trying so hard to pretend a tightness neither of them felt, she tried to respond.

"Oh, well, so far no gray hairs and not too many wrinkles. We'll make it," she laughed, and straightened. "Eat your breakfast, darling, before it gets cold."

He nodded and dug a fork into the little mound of grits, stirring the red gravy from the ham into it, and began eating with an unashamed appetite.

But as she sat opposite him, eating her own breakfast, Lessie saw that the tired lines, the bleakness in his eyes had not been erased. It was a weariness of the spirit far more than of his healthy, strong young body, she knew, and her own heart ached.

"Guess in another few days your road out there will be back to normal," said Ben after he had taken the keen edge of his physical hunger off. "I hear they are going to open up the last leg of the new highway around the lake before the week-end, and then they'll stop using this as a detour."

"That's a day I've been looking forward to for more than six months," admitted Lessie. "I didn't know there were as many cars in the world as go by here every twenty-four hours."

Ben grinned. "And one out of every two or three swears long and loud about having to travel a blankety-blank pig-trail over a mountain in their fancy rich Yankee cars."

"Well, you'll have to admit that's not exactly a highway out there, so you can't really blame them." Lessie turned her head and looked out at the narrow, winding dirt and gravel road that climbed over the mountainside and descended into the valley where the government-sponsored dam had brought such awe-inspiring changes to this peaceful backwater.

Ben was watching her gravely, an odd look in his brown eyes.

"You lived in town awhile, Lessie," he said unexpectedly. "Ever think you'd like to go back there to live?"

Lessie stared at him, wide-eyed and shocked.

"Live in town? Goodness, Ben, no! I'd hate it. I'm mountain stock, born and bred. Why, I'd die in a town, away from here."

Ben gave her his slow, gentle smile that twisted her heart.

"I feel that way, too," he admitted. "I guess you have to be born in the mountains, like us, to really learn to know and love them."

"Like us," she said softly, and their hands clung together.

Chapter 2

Upstairs there was a heavy thump, and then a boy's voice, shouting lustily, "Hi, you loafers! Great gittin'-up time in the mornin'! Rise and shine, kids; rise and shine."

Ben and Lessie exchanged a smile, listening as heavy footsteps thumped across the upstairs hall and into the other rooms, still shouting.

"He has a gentle manner that reminds me of a top-sergeant I had in Korea," murmured Ben with a twinkle in his eyes. "We all loved him devotedly, of course, and made book on the likelihood of him being shot — in the back — the first time he led us into action. But when we actually got into action we were all so busy keeping ourselves alive we forgot we hated the big Mick."

After a short time, feet thundered down the stairs, and Jim Howell, seventeen and big for his age, thrust his way into the kitchen as though pushing aside obstacles invisible to anyone else. His lean, bony young face lightened as he saw Ben.

"How's the boy, Ben?" he demanded.

"Swell, Jim," Ben answered. "I was just telling Lessie that hearing you get those kids out of bed and started toward breakfast reminds me of a top-kick I had in the Army."

Jim accepted it gratefully as a compliment. "Tough guy, eh? You have to get tough with these kids or they'd run Lessie ragged. Believe me, when I yell, they jump!"

"So do I," Lessie admitted, putting his breakfast before him and patting his shoulder affectionately. "Who wouldn't?"

The other children were clattering down the stairs and into the kitchen. Mary Sue, who was fifteen and pretty with the prettiness of all young things; Clyde, twelve and hating his name so much he insisted on being called Butch; and Ellie, the baby, not quite seven.

"I wanted my teacher to see my wish book dress," she whined.

"Miss Clarke can see it Sunday when you go to Sunday School," Lessie tried to comfort her.

"But I *wanted* — " whined Ellie.

"Break it up, break it up," snapped Jim so savagely that Ellie quieted and looked at him with hot, angry eyes. "Boy, will I ever be glad when I'm eighteen and I can get away from all this morning hullabaloo and into the Army! I just hope they keep the wars going another month or two!"

"*Jim!*" Lessie's eyes were blazing, and her tone was one the children seldom heard.

"Oh, sure, sure, I know it's rugged and tough," he answered. "But I also know there are a lot of places I want to see. And I could make Lessie an allotment to help her take care of the kids. Think I don't want to help her handle the responsibilities here, so you two can get married?"

Lessie gave him a startled glance and color poured into her tanned young face. Her eyes turned toward Ben, who gave her his warm, adoring grin that she loved. Jim nodded.

"Don't look surprised," Jim advised. "Gollies, don't you think I've got any sense? Don't you suppose a guy with eyes in the back of his head could take one look at you two and know that you want to get married? But with us kids on Lessie's hands and your Mom and Delsie for you to look after — well, for Pete's sake!"

"You don't have to enlist in the Army and march off to war, Jim, for Lessie and me to be married, you know," Ben pointed out.

"Well, maybe not, but don't say it wouldn't help," Jim insisted stubbornly.

"Now I think it's time for you all to scat and get ready for school before you miss the bus and have to walk!" Lessie said firmly.

When they had clattered up the stairs, Ben smiled tenderly at Lessie.

"Better get started if I'm ever going to get to headquarters. Be seein' you, Honey," he said, and was gone.

Lessie sat for a long moment at the disordered table, her face in her hands, before at last she stood up, giving herself a little shake, and went briskly to work clearing the table.

Chapter 3

It was early afternoon when she came out of the back door, carrying a heavy basket of laundry ready for the clothesline. As she put down the basket and straightened, she paused for a moment to feast her eyes on the picture of spring that the mountains spread before her enchanted eyes.

How, she wondered, drawing a deep breath of the fragrance, feasting her eyes on the beauty around her, could anybody ever want to live anywhere else than here?

She had been so absorbed that she had not heard the sound of a car coming down the drive and she was startled when a man's voice spoke behind her. She turned swiftly.

"I'm sorry. Did I startle you?" He was hatless, tall, his dark red hair ruffled by the light breeze, his blue-green eyes taking her in with eager appreciation of the picture she made against the spring beauty that surrounded her. "I had no idea the mountains could be so beautiful this early in spring."

"Old Baldy and Big Lonesome shield us from the worst of the cold weather, here in

High Valley," she answered, smiling. "That's why spring comes here earlier than in most places around."

"I'm Angus MacDonnell," he introduced himself, and held out his hand, smiling.

"I'm Lessie Howell," she answered, and his hand closed firmly on hers, his smile warm and eager.

"I've been admiring that magnificent old barn across the road," he explained. "I was wondering if it belonged to this property."

"Grandsir's barn? Why, yes, it does. That and the pasture are part of the Howell place."

Magnificent old barn? Well, for goodness' sake! she thought.

"Would your family be interested in renting it? Just for the summer, I mean," he asked.

"Renting it?" she gasped. "For heaven's sake, what *for?*"

"A summer theatre," he admitted, and watched her with surprising intensity as she turned the thought in her mind.

"A theatre?" she gasped. "Way out here in the country? Why, it's miles to town — "

"It's only three or four miles from the Dam," he pointed out. "There are a lot of summer cottages being built there. Lots of people are coming up for the fishing, and there's already a yacht club there and several new motels, and others are breaking out like a rash all along the highway to Atlanta. By the first of June, there'll be a great many people spending vacations at the lake, but there's very little amusement for the evenings. Fishing, boating and swimming are daytime amusements. I'm convinced that a really good summer stock company putting on fairly new Broadway shows, with professional actors, would pay very well. I've been scouting around for a location I felt would be right, and your barn strikes me as a perfect spot. Plenty of parking space in the meadow, far enough from the main highway to keep down traffic noises. Now all I have to do is persuade your father to rent it to me. Or perhaps your husband."

"My father died five years ago, and I'm not married."

"Then you're the head of the household?"

She laughed. "That's what it says on legal papers and income tax blanks," she admitted.

Angus looked swiftly about him. There was not another house in sight. To him, born and bred in a crowded far-flung city, it seemed an unbearably lonely place.

"Don't tell me you live here all alone?" he protested.

"Goodness, no! There are five of us; I have two younger brothers and two sisters.

They are at school now."

"Then may I see the barn? Inside, I mean. That is, if you'd consider renting it to me this summer?" he asked her, his eyes eager.

Lessie studied him curiously.

"It's just a barn you know," she pointed out. "A place for cattle and for their feed. It's got stalls and feed-bins and — honestly, I don't see how it could possibly be used for anything else."

"Well, may we investigate anyway? What did you call it — Grandsir's barn? And why do you call it that?"

They walked down the lane past his good-looking convertible with its New York license plates, as Lessie explained:

"My grandfather came here from Pennsylvania in 1840. That is, he was my great-grandfather. He and my grandmother, who was his bride then, made the trip in a covered wagon, leading a cow and hauling all their worldly possessions. Food, and seed for the crops they were going to plant, and my grandmother brought cuttings of shrubbery and plants and flower-seeds. Those lilacs grew from the cuttings she brought with her, and there's a rose-bush that is still blooming from a cutting she put out."

They soon reached the barn and stood in the huge double doorway that had been designed to accept a two-horse wagon, laden to the top with hay to be pitchforked into the loft.

Lessie watched the man, puzzled, even somewhat amused at his frank excitement, his rapidly growing enthusiasm as he poked and pried into every corner of the old barn. He was explaining to her puzzled and uncomprehending ears the vast possibilities of the place as a summer theatre, and Lessie, who had never in her life seen a stage production, had very slight understanding, though she listened politely.

"What a back-drop!" Angus breathed when they reached the farther end, and she knew he was merely speaking his thoughts aloud. "With the stage here, and those doors swung open to a summer night, and the stars and moon and the mountains — glory, what a scene!"

He turned to Lessie at last, his gray-green eyes shining.

"It's perfect;" he said at last, his tone touched with awe. "Absolutely perfect. I couldn't ever hope to find a better spot. Now all we have to do is agree on a fair rental price. What would you think it would be worth, say from now until the week after Labor Day?"

"I wouldn't know, Mr. MacDonnell. It's

only an old barn!"

"I'll give you three hundred dollars for the season."

Lessie gasped, wide-eyed.

"Three hundred dollars?" she repeated, dazed.

His jaw hardened and his eyes cooled slightly.

"There will be considerable expense involved, Miss Howell, in re-modeling the place into a suitable theatre," he reminded her. "I am not a rich man. However, I very much want the place as I've let you see. I might go as high as four hundred, I suppose — "

Flushed, protesting, Lessie flung out a hand in a silencing gesture as she answered, "Goodness, Mr. MacDonnell, I was trying to tell you that three hundred is too much!"

Startled, Angus frowned down at her.

"You're trying to tell me you'll accept less?" he asked.

"But of course! Goodness, there isn't a family in High Valley who has three hundred dollars cash money in a year! I've never even seen that much money at one time," she confessed honestly.

He laughed at her, all his momentary resentment wiped out by her straightforward honesty.

"Well, I feel three hundred for the season is a very fair price, and am more than willing to pay it, if you'll rent to me," he told her. "Are you going to, Miss Howell? Please, ma'am, may I turn Grandsir's barn into the Old Barn Theatre for three months?"

"Of course," said Lessie. "But three hundred dollars is too much. You may have it for two — if you don't think that's too much. To be honest with you, I do!"

He studied her for a moment, and then he sighed and shook his head.

"I'm wondering what the coming of so-called 'civilization' is going to do to your people in High Valley, Miss Howell! This honesty of yours, setting your price a hundred dollars below what you know I'm willing to pay, instead of upping the price because you know how much I want the place, is very unusual, you know — or *do* you?"

"I don't know anything but that I feel two hundred dollars is an awful lot of money and if I took more I'd be cheating you," she assured him crisply.

"When can you ride in town with me and have a lawyer draw up a lease?" he asked then.

Puzzled, Lessie asked, "But why should we have a lawyer to draw up a lease? I don't need one. But of course if you're afraid to take my word for it — "

"My dear girl," Angus spoke warmly, "I'd take your word if you told me black was white. I'd just feel that anyone who insisted it wasn't was mistaken, that's all."

When Angus had gone in search of carpenters and timber and supplies for the re-modeling, she sat for an unaccustomed moment on the wide front steps of the old house, looking down across the steep slope across the road, down which cars were still whizzing in clouds of dust. Angus had been shocked at her timid question about what he planned to do with the outside of the barn and had assured her firmly that he wouldn't touch it for the world. He had said it was "quaint and picturesque."

Just what having a summer theatre here on the old Howell place was going to mean to the community of High Valley she couldn't imagine. But what two hundred dollars, in cash, was going to mean to her family was a dizzying thought and one that held her silently reflective and somewhat awed.

Chapter 4

About noon the next day she heard a car in the lane and went out to meet Angus, who was getting out of his car, followed by a tall, lean, dark man in well-laundered khaki work-pants and shirt.

"Hi, Lessie." Angus was in high good humor. "This is Lester Dolan who's going to boss the remodeling job on the barn. He'll bring some men up tomorrow, eight or ten if he can get them, for I'm anxious to get the work finished as soon as I can. I'm anxious to get my cast assembled and rehearsals started."

"How do you do, Mr. Dolan?" Lessie's smile was pleasant and friendly. "You don't live in the Valley, I know, because I don't recall having met you before."

The man's homely dark face was touched with a derisive grin.

"No, I'm from Atlanta. Came up here on a job two, three months ago, and when it was finished, another one turned up; looks like I'll be here all summer."

Angus looked out at the narrow green valley

and at the tall blue-gray mountains that enclosed it and at the silvery veil of the waterfall tumbling down the sheer rock face of Old Baldy so that from here it was like a thin white curtain.

"You could spend a summer in worse places, Dolan. Me, I'm looking forward to it."

"Oh, sure, it's a nice enough place," Dolan agreed. "But a fellow like me misses his family. I've got a wife and a couple of kids and I like to be with them nights, not just week-ends. Just going home week-ends doesn't make up for missing so much of seeing the two kids growing up."

"I can understand that," Lessie agreed with him. "I'd be lost without my brood."

"I've been hoping I could find a place to bring the wife and kids up later on, after school's out," Dolan told her, and then he added quickly, "Look, Miss Howell, do you know of any place around here where my men could get a good hot noonday meal? Driving back to the village every day for dinner is going to be a nuisance and take up a lot of time. We work hard, and the men ought to be able to spend their lunch hour resting, not fighting traffic and bad roads five miles each way. But we all need good hot food."

He hesitated, and before Lessie could answer, he asked frankly, "I don't suppose there's any chance you could serve 'em dinner, Miss Howell? We'd be glad to pay well, of course."

"Oh, now see here," Angus cut in swiftly, annoyed. "I promised Miss Howell if she'd rent me the barn I wouldn't let my crowd bother her."

"Sorry," said Dolan apologetically. "It's just that I thought most of the people up here seem glad enough to pick up a few extra bucks along the way."

Lessie was hesitant but excited. After all, she loved to cook. The farm produced its own food; there was a cellar full of canned food she and Mary Sue had put up last summer and fall, and in another month the vegetable garden would begin producing again. There were plenty of fryers coming along in the chicken yard; meat, too, for they had cured hams and smoked bacon and sausage last fall when the two big hogs were butchered.

"If you think your men would be satisfied with just plain country cooking, Mr. Dolan, I'd be glad to try it," she decided at last. "We could try it for a few days, and then if they were not satisfied — "

"There's no question of that, Miss Howell.

The men are getting pretty darned tired of burned hamburgers and half-cooked hot dogs and steak so tough you can't stick a fork in the gravy! They'll be tickled simple to have whatever you want to dish out. We'll make it a trial arrangement, and if you're not satisfied, then we'll move out. O.K.? Is it a deal?"

"It's a deal," Lessie laughed, and put her hand in his.

Angus was looking on, offering no further protest, his expression thoughtful. He turned and surveyed the house: a big, shapeless, rambling old place that had literally grown with the family until the house had finally outgrown the family that was left. Rooms on either side of the main house were long in disuse, because only the central portion was required for Lessie and the children.

"That gives me an idea," he said then. Dolan and Lessie looked puzzled. "I promised to get Dolan back to his present job as soon as he'd looked things over out here. But would you mind if I came out later, Lessie, perhaps after dinner? I'm leaving for New York in the morning and I'd like to discuss this sudden idea with you and the whole family."

"Of course," Lessie smiled. "Come and have supper with us. Then you'll be able to warn Mr. Dolan and his friends what to expect."

"I've already a pretty good idea what they can expect." Dolan chuckled. "And it's too good for 'em, but they're sure going to love it."

Supper was a pleasant meal, with the children much impressed by Angus, while he exerted himself to be an amusing and interesting guest. Afterwards, while Mary Sue and the others, under her authority, cleared the table and washed the dishes, Lessie and Angus sat on the front steps, watching the moonrise over Old Baldy's humped shoulder.

"Funny," said Angus after a long moment of contented silence. "I'm city-bred; always lived in a big city. I get nervous and uncomfortable when I'm away from paved streets, taxis and street lamps. But somehow, out here I'm perfectly contented."

"Oh, that's only temporary. It'll wear off," Lessie teased him. "It's the novelty of it. You'll get awfully tired of country living before the summer is over."

"I hope so." His tone was unexpectedly dry. "I'd hate to think of trying to run a theatre in the Old Barn Theatre in winter. And that's the only way I know to make a living. It means an awful lot to me, Lessie, for this summer to be a success. I'm just about staking my whole future on it, to say nothing of my bank-roll. So it had better pay off."

Before she could speak, he straightened and faced her.

"I told you I had a sudden idea this afternoon, but I kept putting it off for fear you'd be annoyed or resentful," he said as though he had to talk fast before losing his courage. "But there's no sense in stalling any longer. I thought since you are willing to feed Dolan's crowd once a day, you might not mind taking on the company after we get into rehearsals. Only for a midday meal, of course. We'll be working hard, and it would save a lot of time if the company could do as Dolan's crowd will be doing: just across the road and have lunch and relax an hour."

"If you think they will be satisfied by what I offer them, yes, of course. But hadn't we better wait and see whether Mr. Dolan's men are satisfied first?"

"That goes without saying," Angus assured her. "If I say they eat here, instead of wasting time running off to town, they eat here and that's that. They'll be tickled to death, though. I'm sure of that."

He held out his hand, and Lessie laughed

and put hers in it, and they smiled at each other in the moonlight. It was at that moment that the headlights of a car coming up the lane fell full upon them and they looked up, startled. For a moment they were pinned in the beam of those lights against the darkness behind them, and then the car moved on and the light was gone.

"Why, that sounds like Ben's car." Lessie rose as the motor was switched off and the car door slammed.

A moment later Ben came striding across the lawn toward them, as Lessie came to meet him. Angus merely rose and stood where he was.

"Hi, there." To Lessie's ears, Ben's voice had a faint note of strain. "I just stopped off for a moment on my way home from the station."

"I'm so glad you did." Lessie tucked her hand through his arm and was puzzled by its rigidity as she had been puzzled by the slight strain in his voice. "I've been wanting you to meet Mr. MacDonnell. This is Ben Logan, my fiancé."

The two men shook hands briefly, and Ben said, his voice drawling deliberately, "I've been hearing a lot about you."

"None of it too incriminating, I hope," Angus retorted lightly.

"I'm afraid that's a matter of opinion," Ben answered. "Just that you are planning to bring civilization, so-called, to High Valley."

Lessie, puzzled by the taut voices of the two men, looked from one to the other. But the old lilac hedge, fragrant and feathery in the moonlight, cast a shadow on their faces so that she could only guess at their expressions, though their voices told her they did not like each other over much.

"So-called, I'm afraid, is right," Angus admitted. "A summer stock theatre. But I think the building of the dam, the lake area becoming a summer resort and the very fine access roads through formerly inaccessible areas of the Valley are more responsible for the inroads of so-called civilization than my Old Barn Theatre."

"You may be right," Ben drawled, his voice untouched by any warmth. "From what I've seen of what's lightly known as civilization, I'm inclined to be a bit jealous of the invasion of the peace of the valley."

"You'd rather the people went on using coal-oil lamps and knowing little or nothing of what goes on in the outside world?" Angus spoke politely, but his tone was as devoid of warmth and friendliness as Ben's had been all along.

"People have been living here for more than a hundred years and I haven't noticed any of them suffering from a real lack of anything the outside world could bring them." Ben's tone was hard.

Angus made a slight gesture that suggested a shrug.

"Well, I hope you won't feel the summer theatre has harmed anyone's morals by the time the season ends."

"It will be a short season if I figure there's any danger of that," Ben assured him.

"Naturally, I expected that." Angus laughed and turned to Lessie. "Well, I'll be running along. I'll be gone a couple of weeks; I'll see you when I get back. Good night, Mr. Logan. I'll see you around, I hope."

"You may count on that," Ben promised him.

"Oh, I do, I do," Angus responded. A moment later he drove away.

Lessie turned to Ben as the convertible went down the lane and said, "Ben, what got into you? Why were you so rude to Mr. MacDonnell?"

"I don't like the guy!"

"Well, how could you? You'd never met him until tonight. You don't even know him. But I do, and I like him."

Ben looked down at her, and though the

lilac hedge still shadowed his face, she knew from the tone of his voice exactly how it looked: like an Indian mask, cold and set, slow anger burning in his dark eyes.

"Could be that's why I don't like him," he pointed out.

Lessie's eyes widened and she stared at him through the fragrant darkness.

"Why, Ben Logan, I do believe you're jealous! Oh, but you can't be!"

"Can't I? You want to bet?"

A small bubble of laughter escaped Lessie.

"Oh, you blessed idiot! That's the silliest thing I ever heard in all my life. You, jealous of Angus MacDonnell because of me!"

"What's silly about it? You're a lovely girl — "

She put her arms about him and rested her head on his chest.

"You think so, darling, and I love you for it. But Angus MacDonnell! Why, Ben, he's a big theatrical producer. He's city folks; big cities like New York and Hollywood and Miami, I suppose. Golly, Ben, he must know scads of women like those Mary Sue reads about in the movie magazines she trades with her school pals. Glamorous, exciting, alluring women! Why, he'd never look at me — not in the way you're thinking."

"And that bothers you, doesn't it?" asked Ben.

Lessie stared at him, puzzled.

"Bothers me?" she repeated, with no idea of his meaning.

"He's a man, good-looking, smooth and all that. It bothers you that he doesn't notice how beautiful you are — "

"Oh, for heaven's sake, Ben!" Her tone was caught between laughter and exasperation. "Why, darling, he's old! He must be somewhere between thirty-five and forty! And he's a flat-lander, darling. You can't possibly believe that I'd care what a flat-lander, even one as nice as Angus MacDonnell, thinks about me? Ben, darling, how foolish can you be? And besides, I love you! I have no room in my heart for even a thought of another man."

He drew her close into his arms and held her for a long moment. Beneath her cheek she could feel the hard, uneven pounding of his heart and there was a mist of tears in her eyes. They were so in love, and the future when they could belong to each other seemed so far away.

He put her away from him at last, and looked down at her.

"You know something? We came darned near a quarrel." His voice was touched with the solemnity of the thought.

Lessie laid her cheek for a moment against his hand where it rested on her shoulder.

"We couldn't ever really quarrel, Ben. I could no more quarrel with you than with myself. I couldn't hurt you deliberately without hurting myself more, because you are a part of me, dearest."

"Sure." Ben's voice was husky with tenderness. "It's like that with me, too. But when I drove up just now and saw you sitting here in the moonlight holding hands with him, it hit me hard right where I live."

"You blessed silly, I wasn't holding hands with him," Lessie laughed. "I was shaking hands with him, over a deal we had closed."

"What sort of deal? He's already got the barn; what more does he want, for Pete's sake?"

"You probably won't like it," she warned him. "But I'm going to serve a noon-day meal to the carpenters working on re-modeling the barn, and then when the troupe gets here, I'm going to serve them lunch."

Ben bristled. "You're darn right I don't like it! It will work you to death — "

"Oh, pooh!" She dismissed that as of no consequence whatever. "I've always worked hard and I like it. School will be out next week, Mary Sue and Jim will be here to help me, and Butch will look after Ellie. Why, it'll be a breeze! And it will give me some money to put away for the winter, when we'll all need it."

Ben had walked with her to the steps, where they sat now as she had sat with Angus. Slowly, methodically, Ben filled his pipe and had it going before he spoke.

He was looking out over the mountains, a magnificent sweep of silvery moonlight and blue-black shadows. The meadow surrounding the old barn was awash with moonlight, and the old barn seemed to float like some sturdy, ungainly old ship in that silver-blue sea.

"Sure, we're all going to make piles and piles of money out of the summer people now that the road is open; but I'm wondering if it will repay us for all we will have lost," he said slowly at last.

Lessie laid her cheek against his shoulder, her hands locked about his arm.

"I don't think we can ever keep things the way they used to be, Ben," she admitted. "Progress sort of comes along and rolls over us whether we like it or not. We just have to go along with it, and adapt ourselves as best we can and take comfort from the thought that the next generation will benefit by it."

"Sure, sure, Honey." Ben nodded, and she heard him sigh. "Looks as if we might be having to do a lot of adjusting and adapting. There's a wild scramble on by the summer people to buy up 'quaint old farmhouses' that have housed a hundred years of simple living and turn them into summer homes, to be used a month, two or three, during the year and locked up to stand idle the rest of the year."

He looked down at her in the moonlight.

"You could get a pretty fancy price for the old Howell place, Lessie," he said quietly.

She gasped in outrage. "Sell my home? The children's home? Ben, you don't know what you're saying. Why, Grandsir would turn over in his grave."

"You can't keep thinking about what *they* would want, Lessie. It's your place now. You could get enough to take the kids to town and give them advantages — "

"Ben, do you honestly think the children would be better off in town?" Her voice was tense now and she was deeply in earnest. "Don't you feel with me that they have a better chance of growing up into decent, honest law-abiding citizens right here? Don't you think they have a better chance for a happy, normal childhood here, where the family's roots are? Where they have a feeling of belonging? Ben, I'd smother to death cooped up in a city place so close to neighbors that I'd only have to sniff real hard to know what they were having for supper. I've got to have elbow room and that's what I want the children to have, at least until they are old enough to make a choice for themselves."

Ben's laugh was warm and tender with relief.

"That's what I hoped you'd say, Lessie," he admitted. "I know how ambitious you are for the children, and I was afraid you'd feel it was in their best interests for you to sell out and leave. And whether you wanted to or not, if you felt it was best for them, you're such a conscientious little goof, you'd do it."

"I guess I would," she agreed. "But I don't feel it is, so you can stop worrying. I'm here, and here I stay. It's a good life, Ben, the mountains. It's my life. I would ask no better."

He stood up then and knocked out his pipe, assuring himself the last tiny spark had been ground into ashes in the gravelled walk, with the inborn care and caution that made him so good at his job. He bent his head, kissed her lightly without putting his arms about her, and drove away, taking with him the picture of her as she stood there, straight and slender, with the moonlight making a halo about her proudly held dark head.

Chapter 5

Monday morning brought Mr. Dolan and his crew and truckloads of lumber and supplies. Lessie stood on the front porch watching them unload the trucks, hearing their voices brought to her by the crisp morning air. There was an air of confusion about the scene, but reason told her it was only seeming confusion.

Two of the men came over shortly before noon and spread clean wide planks on two saw-horses beneath the old oak trees in the back yard, and one of them held out a large box.

"Dolan said the thing his wife minded most about having a big crowd to feed was washing the dishes afterward, so he thought maybe you'd better use these paper plates and stuff and then just burn the whole thing when dinner's over," he explained.

He stood for a minute looking out over the magnificent sweep of mountains, and then he said, "Mighty pretty place you've got here. Bet it gets right lonesome some times, though. And mighty cold in winter, too."

"There's not much time to be lonesome." Lessie laughed. "I have a brood of brothers and sisters to take care of. But it does get cold in winter, I'll admit."

"Still, there's plenty of wood around, I suppose. Nothing like a big open log fire on a cold night." He smiled and said, "Guess I'd better be getting back to work before Dolan starts yelling for me."

He walked away, and Lessie called Mary Sue to help her get the big table ready. She had dreaded the first few days, but she was surprised to discover that they settled swiftly into a routine that she and Mary Sue and Jim were able to handle without undue stress.

"It's working out beautifully," Lessie told Ben, when he stopped by at the end of the first week. "The men like my cooking, and they are so friendly and pleasant; and not having to wash dishes after a meal helps a lot on the work. I like it!"

Ben smiled at her as he sat across the supper table from her, drinking the cup of coffee she had insisted on pouring for him.

"You're the kind that likes being worked to death," he teased.

Lessie laughed. "Do I look worked to death?"

"You look beautiful and radiant as you

always do." Ben's voice sobered, and then he said quickly, "Had a letter from Delsie today. She's going to stay on this summer and take a special course, instead of coming home for the summer."

Lessie felt her heart slide down.

"But, Ben, she's needed here — " she began, and then checked the words swiftly.

"She says by taking the summer course she won't have to go back next winter. She'll be ready to teach by the time school opens up here in October," Ben pointed out. His eyes shone and there was a warmth in them that seemed to bathe Lessie in tenderness.

"Oh, Ben," she whispered, awed by the sudden hope. "Does that mean — "

"It means the waiting is nearly over, Honey." Ben's voice was low-pitched and not quite steady. "With Delsie at home, and with me looking in on Mother every day, there's no reason why we can't be married. By Christmas, anyway."

Lessie sat very still, but her heart was leaping within her. Not until now, when it seemed that their waiting was to be a matter of months instead of years, had she dared to dream of being married to Ben. Oh, some day, of course — but so far away. But now, with Delsie at home, they could actually begin making plans!

"Oh, Ben," she whispered, her voice shaking. She put her hand in his, and for a long moment they sat there, awed and uplifted by the sudden upward surging of their hope. . . .

It was mid-afternoon when Lessie heard a sudden clamor of car horns and saw several cars driving in at the barn, and people tumbling out. She recognized Angus' convertible, and there was a dark green sedan, and a well-kept Ford.

She waited, watching as they all trooped through the barn where the work had almost been completed. Then they came back across the road, Angus' convertible leading the way.

"Hi, there!" he greeted Lessie with a joyous exuberance, and turned to the woman who had sat beside him. "Teresa, this is Lessie; Lessie, this is Teresa."

The woman smiled at Lessie, and the smile lit her plain face to something approaching beauty. She was small and neatly tailored, and save for the mass of auburn curls that framed her face, she barely escaped being homely.

"Hello, Lessie. Andy's been telling me some fabulous stories about you, and about this place, but I'm beginning to believe he was telling no more than the simple truth. It's a heavenly place," she said, and her voice was the most beautiful Lessie had ever heard: like the chiming of small golden bells, each one in perfect tune.

"Tell me I'm the luckiest fellow in the world to have charmed her out of retirement and back to work," beamed Angus, his arm around the woman's shoulders. "Half the producers on Broadway would give their eye-teeth for her name on a contract; yet *I'm* the fellow that's got it."

"Dear Andy," said Teresa softly, and patted his cheek lightly. "And Lessie, this is Carolyn Somers, my oldest and best friend."

She turned and held out her hand to the elderly, comfortably plump woman who had shared the front seat of Angus' car with her.

"Hello, Lessie," said Carolyn, and looked around her. "If I needed to prove I'm her best friend, I've done it by coming here for the summer. You sure all the Indians are gone, Lessie?"

"Oh, a long time ago," Lessie laughed, and knew she was going to like this woman very much.

Two young people were climbing out of the rumble seat of Angus' car, and he smiled at the fragile, lovely blonde in a smartly cut jade-green suit, with no hat on her shimmering pale gold hair.

"Jane Ellerbe, Lessie, and Howard England, two of my apprentices," Angus introduced them, smiling.

"How do you do?" said Jane, her voice low and throaty.

"Hi." Howard was boyishly charming. "I haven't seen so much space since Cinerama. Playing here is certainly going to be different. I just hope nobody gets too enthusiastic at rehearsals and tosses his opponent off a cliff!"

The dark green sedan had come to a halt behind the convertible, and a tall, darkly handsome young man was getting out, turning to extend his hand to his companion, a girl of twenty-two or three, with chestnut brown hair and eyes that were almost amber. The man's hand on hers, his eyes that smiled at her, met the adoration in her own as she thanked him and tucked her hand through his arm and turned to face the others.

"And here are our honeymooners," Angus introduced them, "Jon and Lucy Blair. Jon is our leading man, and Lucy — "

She laughed and finished for him, "Came along for the ride, of course. I'm probably the world's worst actress, but I offered to scrub the stage or paint scenery if Andy would let me come along with Jon."

"That's not true. She's a wonderful actress!" Jon protested.

Lucy laughed. "Remind me to show you

my clippings, sometime — both of them. Especially the one that said, 'Lucy Cole was adequate as the younger sister — but only barely.' "

"By the time the season here is over, you'll be an actress, and a darned good one. MacDonnell, the Star-Maker himself, in person." Jon bowed with mocking deference toward Angus, who merely grinned.

"And here's Mason Lawrence, our heavy, and Carlton James, who does characters." Angus turned to the two men who were approaching, one an elderly man with thick, snow-white hair and twinkling blue eyes; the other a stockily built, powerful-looking younger man whose dark, homely face now wore a friendly grin. "Where are Elaine and Jud?" asked Angus.

"Down at the theatre, naturally," answered the older man, Carlton James, smiling as he gave Lessie an old-fashioned, formal bow. "Those kids are so in love with the smell of grease paint and the glare of footlights they can't wait for rehearsals."

He indicated the dark man beside him, and went on, "Don't let Mason frighten you, my dear. He looks violently wicked, but I assure you that offstage he's as mild as milk and as meek as a lamb. Completely harmless, in fact."

"If you were twenty years younger, I'd stuff those words down your throat," Mason said pleasantly. "A more scathing denunciation it would be impossible to imagine than presenting a man to a charming lady as 'completely harmless.' I resent it bitterly. Hello, Miss Howell."

"I have to admit I'm not a bit terrified of you, Mr. Lawrence," Lessie admitted, laughing, liking these people, finding them exciting and intriguing.

"Wait until you see me twirl my black mustachios and crack my bull-whip, with my wide-brimmed black hat dragged down over my wicked eyes," Mason warned gently.

"I hadn't planned to do 'Uncle Tom's Cabin' this season, Mason," Angus protested, laughing.

"No matter. I can be just as terrifying as the mad scientist or even the creature from outer space. Incidentally, why don't we do *Dracula*? That's a make-up I love."

"Not this season, thanks," grinned Angus.

Teresa said softly, "A roll of drums, please, and a flourish of trumpets. The Lily Maid approaches, with captive swain in tow. I wonder what she'd look like without a man on her arm. I'll never know, for nobody's ever going to see that."

Angus said under his breath, anxiety in

his tone, "Please, darling — I'm sorry you hate her so, but she was the best I could get for second leads."

"If she'll be satisfied with second leads — which, of course she won't — I'll promise to keep my dagger out of her back. But one false move and I'll let her have it!" threatened Teresa ominously.

By now the two had reached the group and Lessie saw that the well-scrubbed, crew-cut young man had a slightly dazed expression as though just slowly coming out of a coma, while the girl beside him was the most beautiful creature Lessie had ever seen. Her hair was the rich, ripe gold of wheat ready for harvesting, and her skin had the almost translucent quality of flower petals. She wore no make-up save geranium-red lipstick, and her frock was deceptively simple, but even to Lessie's eyes it had a look of being expensive.

"This is the most fabulous place, Mr. MacDonnell." Her voice was low, throaty, carefully placed, and her smile was warm on Angus. "It's going to be a wonderful experience working here with you. I can't tell you how lucky I feel."

Lessie caught the derision that touched Teresa's face briefly as Angus answered the girl pleasantly.

"I hope you'll find it so, Elaine. Your company was very anxious that you have this summer stock experience before you returned to Hollywood. I hope you won't find it too difficult. Summer stock is hard work."

Her eyes caressed him.

"Oh, but I shan't mind a bit, Mr. Mac-Donnell. I'm so lucky to be working with you," she said sweetly.

"Well, we'd all better be getting back to town and settled in," said Angus, rounding them up with his eyes. "First rehearsal at nine-thirty in the morning and we open a week from Tuesday. So let's get going."

When they had all gone save Angus, Teresa and Carolyn, Teresa turned to Angus, and Lessie was startled to see tears in the dark brown eyes.

"Angus, please let me stay here a little while. It's the most peaceful spot I've ever seen," she whispered.

"Teresa, my dear — " Angus caught her hands, but she twisted free and whirled away from him and went running around the house toward the path leading up across the orchard.

"Let her go, Andy." Carolyn's voice was touched with tears. "Coming back to life after you've given it up, as she has, isn't easy. You'll have to be very patient with her."

"All the patience in the world, Caro, you know that." Angus spoke in a troubled tone. "But this deep, brooding grief can't be good for her."

"Can't it? I wonder!" Carolyn's tone was dry. "Don't they say all great artists need to suffer before they can reach the peak of their art? If that's true, then, Andy, she should be greater than Bernhardt. Oh, sure, I know thousands of women have lost husbands they adored. She's not unique, except to you and to me, because she's Teresa and we love her."

Angus asked, "Did I do wrong, Caro, in persuading her to come back to work?"

"Of course not, darling." Caro's tone was swift and comforting. "It's the one thing she needs more than any other. She can use the salary, too."

Angus frowned. "You mean she's short of money?"

Caro chuckled without humor. "I mean she's broke, flat, busted. Been living on her jewelry for the past year. Everything except what Ted gave her, and she'd starve before she'd hock that."

"But I thought — "

"You thought what everybody thought,

what she wanted everybody to think — that she and Ted had scads of money and she need never work again if she didn't want to. Well, she and Ted made scads of money, but they were both of them suckers for a hard luck story. Any panhandler could get the shirt off their backs if they had a good story with which to ask for it. And when she stepped out of the show the night Ted died, she stepped out of a lush salary. She hasn't made a dime in more than two years. So this job is a godsend to her."

"Caro, I didn't dream — "

"Of course not. She didn't want you to. She didn't want anybody to." Caro drew a deep breath. "I could have yelled for joy when she started throwing barbs at the lovely Elaine. I knew then she was beginning to snap back, that she wasn't going just to sit back and let Elaine run barefoot all over her."

"I'll see to that," Angus stated.

Caro grinned at him impishly, her eyes merry, but all she said was "Men!"

Lessie had been looking on, listening, puzzled and uneasy.

Caro caught the expression and suddenly put an arm about Lessie.

"Don't mind us, Lessie," she said cheerfully. "We're nuts, of course, but most show biz people are. Just don't try to understand us; I'm afraid you'll have to take us as we are."

"Why, of course. I think you're wonderful. Only I'm a little confused," admitted Lessie, and joined Caro and Angus in their friendly laughter.

Chapter 6

Teresa paused for breath at last and stood beside the huge old Douglas pine, clinging to its rough, friendly bark as she fought to breathe normally. Her eyes took in the wonderful sweep of scenery before her, and gradually she came back to some small measure of self-control.

"How you would have loved all this, my darling," she whispered. And then grief shook her as a young sapling is shaken in a stormy wind, and she slid down on the thick, spicy carpet of pine-needles and wept bitterly.

She was startled at last by a childish treble voice above her, warm with sympathy and concern. "Did you fall down and hurt yourself?"

Teresa lifted her head and looked straight into an exquisite child's face only a few inches above her own, where the child squatted on her haunches, a ragged, disheveled-looking doll clutched in one arm.

"Oh, hello, Honey, where did you come from?" She managed to sit up and to mop her tear-stained face with an inadequate handkerchief.

"I live here," said the child, rebuke in her tone. "But you don't, do you?"

"You live here?" Teresa looked about her at the loneliness of the scene, with not so much as a wisp of smoke to indicate a dwelling anywhere.

"Not here," rebuked the child. "Down there at the Howell place. I'm Ellie Howell."

"Oh, I met your sister Lessie this afternoon."

Worry brushed fleetingly across the child's lovely face.

"Are you going to tell Lessie I was way up here all by myself?"

Teresa laughed. "Aren't you supposed to be?"

Ellie shook her curls. "I'm supposed to tag along with Butch. Only he got tired of me hanging around and told me to go home. But I knew everybody was busy down at the house and they wouldn't miss me, so I stayed and played pretend."

"Oh, that's a lovely game!"

Ellie's small face became ecstatic.

"Did you ever play pretend?" she asked, awed.

"All my life," said Teresa, and managed to keep her voice steady. "I'm playing pretend right now. I'm pretending that you and I are friends and that we're going to have a lot of fun this summer."

"Oh, that'd be wonderful," glowed Ellie, and then uneasily, "Are you summer people?"

Momentarily puzzled, Teresa laughed. "I'm going to work with Angus MacDonnell at the Old Barn Theatre. Does that make me 'summer people'?"

Ellie shook her head vigorously.

"Oh, no, that means you're show people. Summer people come up and buy up all our houses and things. That's what Ben told Lessie." There was a note of sage wisdom in the small, sweet voice.

Teresa laughed and hugged the child.

"Ellie, you're delightful!"

Ellie beamed happily, and held up her doll.

"I forgot. This is Susie Belle. She's not very pretty, but she's smart as a whip and awful sweet."

Her eyes pleaded with Teresa, who touched the doll gently and said, "Why, I think she's beautiful. A doll you can play with is so much more fun than a fancy-clothes doll you have to just look at."

It was the right answer, she realized when she saw the look in the child's eyes.

Ellie looked up and squinted at the slanting rays of sunlight that were feeling their way through the tops of the huge trees, and sighed.

"I guess it must be late." She stood up. "At least it *looks* like it was late. I'd better be getting on home before I worry Lessie."

"Would she spank you?" asked Teresa, and was instantly sorry.

Ellie's eyes widened with shock and surprise.

"Oh, no, Lessie wouldn't ever spank me! She loves me; and I love her, too, so I don't want to worry her."

Teresa stood up, brushed the needles carelessly from the skirt of her well-cut suit, and held out her hand to Ellie, smiling warmly.

"We'll go down together, darling. I should be getting back, too."

"Will somebody worry about you if you're late?" asked Ellie, skipping along beside Teresa, her small, grubby little paw held tightly in the woman's.

Teresa caught her breath with a stab of pain, and then she tilted her chin and made herself say, "Why, of course. Andy and Caro will worry about me."

"Are they your folks?" asked Ellie, deeply interested.

Teresa bit her lip for a moment to steady

her voice, and then she answered with surface lightness, "Why, yes, they are my folks; they're really more than my folks. They're my very dearest and best friends."

Ellie nodded, perfectly satisfied with that answer, and a little later the two of them came across the path through the orchard.

"There she is," Caro said to Angus, and added, puzzled, "But where did she find the child? Whose child is it?"

"Mine," said Lessie, and went to meet the two. "Where have you been, Ellie?"

Elle looked up and then lowered her eyes.

"With Butch," she answered, the picture of innocence.

"Then where *is* Butch?" Lessie pursued.

"He went fishing, so I came home with this lady."

She lifted wide, imploring eyes to Teresa, whose hand tightened on hers as Teresa smiled winningly at Lessie.

"I suppose I would have gotten myself lost if Ellie hadn't showed me the way back," she said pleasantly.

"You are not supposed to be alone on the mountain," Lessie addressed herself to Ellie.

"Well, it was for just a little while, Lessie. Butch brought me to the path and told me to come straight home, and I would've, only I found the lady up there and we visited for a little and then we came home," Ellie explained virtuously.

"I hope you were not worried about her, Lessie," said Teresa coaxingly.

"I was worried about you," said Caro, a trace of sharpness in her tone.

Teresa, still holding the child's hand, smiled down at her and then at Caro.

"You don't have to worry about me any more Caro." There was a richness in her tone, a look in her eyes that illumined her plain face and gave her a touch of beauty. "You see, I found the way home."

For a moment Caro and Angus exchanged swift, startled glances and then Caro turned away to hide the tears in her eyes.

"That's wonderful news, darling," said Angus, his voice low and not quite steady.

"Dear Andy! Dear Caro!" Teresa's voice was tender. "How you've put up with me these last years I'll never know. But I've got my feet on the ground now, Andy; I can live with my memories and adjust. Sir James M. Barrie knew what he was talking about when he said, 'God gave us memory, so we may have red roses in December.' The thorns have been pretty bad, but now I'm going to concentrate on the roses."

"Swell! That's my girl." Angus bent his head and touched her cheek with his lips.

Teresa stood for a long moment looking out over the panorama before her, and then she turned, suddenly impulsive, to Lessie.

"Would you think me outrageous if I asked you to let me sleep here? To live here and not in the village this summer? Do you have room? Anything will do — "

"Oh, come now, Teresa. I promised Lessie we wouldn't swamp her — "

Teresa wasn't listening. She was looking at Lessie, meeting her eyes straightly, adding no more to her pleas than the heart-touching eloquence in her great dark eyes.

"There's plenty of room, Miss Carr, but this is just a farmhouse. No conveniences or comforts such as you would have in the village — " Lessie began.

"But such peace! Such blessed, incredible peace! If you only knew, Lessie. I hope you never will — but if you could — " Teresa's lovely, bell-like voice broke and stumbled into silence.

"If you want to stay, Miss Carr, we'll do our best to make you comfortable — "

"Teresa, darling, this is crazy," Caro protested.

Teresa smiled at Lessie, and put her hand on Caro's plump arm.

"Would there be room for both of us? We haven't been apart in more than two years. Not even a night. I'm being outrageous, I know, but it means so terribly much to me to be able to live here."

Lessie laughed and made a gesture.

"There are six unoccupied rooms, all furnished in the country fashion — mountain-made furniture and all the rest of it. I'm afraid you won't be very comfortable, but you'll be very welcome."

Teresa gave a little cry of delight and embraced Lessie, and turned, bright-eyed and eager, to Caro.

"Throw away the sleeping pills, Caro," she carolled happily. "I won't need them here."

"In that case, it's worth it," she said, with a smile at Lessie.

Chapter 7

Mary Sue, helping Lessie get supper ready, said, puzzled, "I thought all actresses, especially stars, were beautiful and glamorous. Why, Lessie, Miss Carr's almost homely."

"Well, she's a very fine actress, and if you can really act I guess maybe being beautiful isn't so important. I love her voice, don't you?" said Lessie.

"Golly, yes! It makes tingles run up and down my spine. I bet she's really something on the stage," said Mary Sue, and giggled.

"I can't wait to see Ben's face when he discovers we've taken two summer boarders," Lessie said, acknowledging her faint but growing uneasiness.

Mary Sue looked at her quickly.

"Will he be mad?" she asked. "Just about a couple of women? If it had been that nice young man they call Juddy, or that bee-you-tiful Mr. Blair — "

"Silly! Ben minds only that I'm taking on extra work."

"Oh, well, you don't have to worry about Ben. He's not your husband yet!"

"But he's going to be, Mary Sue. Perhaps by Christmas."

Mary Sue gasped, "Oh, Lessie, really?"

"If Delsie comes home and takes the school at Flat Rock, so she can be at home with her mother at night, it may work out that way."

"Oh, Lessie, I'm so glad for you! Ben's a sweetie-pie and I love him! And you've been so good, taking care of a bunch of kids like us all these years!"

"It's been a pleasure." Lessie was trying for a light tone, but her eyes were warm and eager with dreams. "But it's going to be nice to have Ben around all the time!"

"Well, I should think so!" glowed Mary Sue. "Oh, Lessie, I think it's simply scrumptious! I'm so happy for you both."

Caro appeared at the door, in a crisp cotton frock, saying pleasantly, "Well, give me something to do. I haven't been in a real kitchen in more years than I'd care to admit, and I want to be a help. I'm a marvelous hand at dishwashing and enjoy it."

Mary Sue cried out in sharp protest, "Oh, Mrs. Somers, you *can't* be! Nobody loves to wash dishes! It's — well, it's just not normal."

Caro chuckled. "Whoever said I was normal? If I had been, I'd have got out of show business when I was young; better still, I'd never have got into it in the first place."

Mary Sue asked, "Don't you like show business, Mrs. Somers?"

"What's with this 'Mrs. Somers' routine?" demanded Caro. "I hate that name; and besides, it isn't mine. I only adopted it because it would look good in electric lights. Only unfortunately I never had the chance to find out. I'm Caro — and the first one that says 'Aunt Caro' is going to be smacked, but good! That is, unless it's the infant over there. She can call me, 'Hi, you!' if she wants to. I owe that youngster an awful lot; but you are too young to understand. So put me to work, Lessie. Let's get with it."

"We'll have supper in the dining-room, Mrs. — I mean Caro, so you can set the table." Lessie was slightly flustered by having a stranger in her kitchen.

"Why the dining-room, when you've got such a love of a kitchen?" protested Caro, looking about the big, pleasant, homely place.

"But we couldn't ask Miss Carr to eat in the kitchen!" protested Mary Sue, big-eyed. "Golly, a famous actress like her?"

Caro studied the girl and smiled.

"Teresa is first, last and always a human being; and then an actress and a very fine one," said Caro. Then she lowered her voice, and went on, "I thought perhaps you should know that she's going through a very bad time. About two years ago, her husband died very suddenly. They were utterly devoted to each other. Neither of them had a family, others to rally round when there was trouble. They had tough times, but that only brought them closer together. Gradually, they began to get ahead the most heart-breaking business in the world; Teresa as an actress, Ted as a very fine producer. She was playing the last performance of a very successful run, and Ted had been arranging the road tour. He was driving back from Philadelphia when he had a heart attack. He managed to get the car to the side of the road, and to get out of it. He died in a ditch beside the road."

Lessie cried out, "Oh, how awful!"

"For Teresa, it was the end of everything. She left the stage, crawled into a hole and would see nobody, except me. I'm not easy to avoid. I knew she needed me, even if she didn't think so. The only thing that could ever have dragged her back to living was Andy. He and Ted were close friends; Ted taught Angus what he knows and Angus will never forget his devotion to Ted. Angus is so tied up with Ted in her memories that Teresa consented to come here for this summer. I feel sure that by the time this season is over, she'll be adjusted, back on her feet, willing to admit that her only future is in her work."

She looked swiftly from one concerned, anxious young face to another, and then she smiled, tears misty in her eyes.

"I felt you had the right to know," she said gently, "and to see what I meant when I said the kindest thing you can do for her is take her into your home, your lives, and treat her as you would a friend. Please don't give her the celebrity treatment. It will only hurt her. Accepting her as one of yourselves will make the summer complete for her, and give her the best medicine she could possibly have for the sickness of her heart."

She glanced out of the window and straightened.

"Now who," she demanded, "is that gorgeous hunk of man?"

Puzzled, Lessie followed her glance and felt color come into her face that had nothing to do with the heat from the stove.

"Why," she said, her tone warm, "that's Ben."

"So?" murmured Caro, and eyed her with a twinkle. "Friend of yours, I take it."

"He's the man I'm going to marry," said

Lessie, her tone rich with the thrill of that.

"Lucky Ben!" said Caro, and then with a glance at Lessie, and a smile, "And lucky you! What a couple you'll make."

Ben had come around to the back door, as was his custom at this time of the day, knowing he would find Lessie in the kitchen cooking supper.

"Hello, Honey." His voice was a warm, tender thing that curled like small, gentle fingers about Lessie's young heart, and then he saw Caro and stopped. "Oh, I'm sorry. I didn't know you had company."

"I'm not company," said Caro pleasantly. "I live here, for the summer, anyway. How are you, Ben? I'm Caro. If you want to be formal, which I hope you won't, I'm Carolyn Somers."

"I'm happy to meet you, Mrs. Somers," said Ben stiffly.

"I bet," Caro drawled. "But Teresa and I will try not to be underfoot too much during the summer."

Ben looked at Lessie, and she quailed a little at his glance. Caro, who seemed perfectly content to chatter at length without waiting for anybody to answer her, said, "Now if you'll excuse me — and I'm sure you will — I'll collect Teresa so she can wash her hands and get ready for supper.

Want to go with me, infant?" She held out a hand to Ellie, who scrambled eagerly to her feet and put her small hand in Caro's and led the way out of doors.

Mary Sue, with a swift glance at Ben, who was wearing what his friends called his "Indian mask" that indicated he was "getting up a good mad," murmured something by way of an excuse and managed to get out of the room.

"So now it's summer boarders, as well as all the rest," said Ben, his tone deceptively mild, his eyes accusing.

"If you'd just let me explain — " Lessie began.

"Let you? I insist on it!"

A spark of anger blossomed in Lessie's heart, but she held it down and as briefly and quietly as she could she explained how Teresa and Caro happened to be living with the family. For the time being, she said, and she had no idea how long that would be; possibly for a few days, possibly until the season closed.

"After all, Ben," she finished defiantly, "there are six unoccupied rooms in the house that we don't use at all — "

"Oh, but I'm sure MacDonnell would be glad to stable his entire troupe here if you'd let him know about the vacancies."

"Oh, Ben, please. I'm tired. Let's not fight!"

"Tired? Well, of course you are. Why else have I been trying to keep you from letting yourself in for all this upheaval? Not because I like quarreling with you, you may be sure. Simply because I'd prefer you not to work yourself to death for a few lousy dollars — "

Her look stopped him and for a moment he turned away from her, his hands jammed in his pockets. She thought he meant to leave like that, and cried out his name.

"Ben, Ben, how foolish can you be? Do you think that I'll ever notice the extra work? I haven't exactly loafed, you know, for quite a few years." Her voice was steady, her eyes met his squarely. "I'll cook for these people exactly as I have always cooked for the children and myself; I'll just cook more, that's all. No extra flourishes or fancy things; that was the understanding I had with them all."

Ben hesitated, his back to her, and after a moment she went on quietly, "Ben, darling, if you'd only brush that chip off your shoulder and give yourself a chance really to know these people, you'd find they are very much like ourselves. Don't be stiff-necked and intolerant, Ben. Stop fighting against the goads, and battling the current. This is the way it's going to be up here now; whether you and I like it or not, what you call our privacy and what I call our isolation is being invaded and it will be more and more so as time goes along. Remember the old saying, 'If you can't lick 'em, join 'em.' Please try, Ben — for my sake."

Ben turned then and looked at her, frowning still but with the Indian mask beginning to break up.

"You're right, Honey," he said at last, and her heart leaped at the sound of his voice; not happy, but beginning to accept the inevitable. "I'm the one who's wrong. I have no right to try to boss you around. I guess maybe that's one reason I see red when you do something I don't want you to do."

There were voices outside, and Ben bent swiftly, drew her close in his arms and kissed her.

"Stay for supper, Ben," she begged, as they heard footsteps on the old front porch.

"Thanks, Honey, but Mother is expecting me." Ben's voice was husky with tenderness. "She wants to come and see you one afternoon soon. She knows you are too busy to come to her."

"I'll love having her, Ben, any time at all; you know that."

"Sure I do, Honey. If only we could convince her — but we can't, so there's no use talking about it," said Ben, and Lessie remembered how they had tried to get Mrs. Logan to come and live at the Howell place, so that Ben and Lessie could be married, and how the old lady had rebelled, until at last they knew the utter futility of such persuasion.

Teresa's voice, warm and chiming with the golden bells that Lessie seemed always to hear in her voice, was in the hall now. A moment later, she stood in the kitchen doorway, looking with bright, friendly eyes at Ben.

"Caro told me you were here, Ben. I'm so glad to meet you." She put her hand in Ben's, and Lessie, watching Ben, could see the way he came under Teresa's spell and knew that it must be like that any time Teresa wished it.

"I do hope you won't think we're imposing on Lessie, Ben," said Teresa, and Lessie wondered uneasily if Teresa had overheard some part of the talk she and Ben had had. "She's such a fine person and so good. We won't overwork her, I promise!"

"Not intentionally, I'm sure, Miss Carr," Ben answered.

"You're Ben, and I'm Teresa, please. We'll save the Miss Carr for when I'm on stage, shall we?" Her friendliness was so honest and so straightforward that there was conviction of its utter sincerity in every tone.

"Thanks, Teresa. I'll look forward to seeing you on stage," said Ben.

"Oh, but you mustn't wait until then. Angus wants to give a preview party for everybody who will come, the Saturday night before we open. I hope you'll be there, Ben, and all your friends."

"Thanks, I wouldn't want to miss it," said Ben heartily, and grinned at Lessie, who was beaming at him joyously.

He said goodnight and went out, and Teresa said softly, "You love him very much, don't you, Lessie?"

"With all my heart."

"And he adores you. I'm so glad for you both, Lessie. So very, very glad. Because love is the most perfect thing in the world. Oh, it can hurt you so that you want to die! But loving someone, losing someone — that's the price we pay for belonging. And nobody could want to live without love, no matter how much it hurts when you have to let go."

There was a mist of tears in her eyes and her voice shook, but she turned swiftly away as Caro came bustling in and the moment was lost.

Chapter 8

Angus stood up with a barely controlled impatience and said brusquely, "Break for lunch. Everybody back here at two. Jane, I'd like you to wait a minute, please."

Teresa, her face stormy, turned sharply and went out of the barn, and the others trooped after her, leaving Jane and Angus alone.

Angus perched on the edge of the kitchen table, the blue-covered script folded in nervous, impatient hands. He was controlling himself with an effort, while Jane sat tensely, her hands locked tightly together in her lap, not looking at him.

"Well, Jane?" Angus said at last. "What's the matter?"

Jane looked up at him fearfully and then away.

"I don't know, Angus. I just can't seem to — well, to feel it."

"You realize, of course, that you're killing the scene?"

"Oh, I couldn't do that, Angus. My part is too small."

"My dear girl, there *are* no small parts — only small actresses."

Jane lowered her shining blonde head, and her hands were so tightly clenched that the base of the nails was white.

"I'm sorry," she whispered helplessly.

"That's not going to do us much good, Jane, unless you can pull yourself together and get on with it." Angus was still holding himself under control, but some of his impatience and resentment edged his tone. "The scene is an important one. Oh, sure, it only covers a couple of 'sides' in your script; just the same, in that scene Teresa is building up to a big moment in the play that will carry over into the other two acts. And we've got to establish the point in this scene with her younger sister. And you're not helping. You're feeding her the lines cold; you're not helping her work up to the scene she has the minute you leave the stage. The way you're playing the scene is unforgivable. I'm surprised, Jane. You're much better than your work in this scene indicates."

Jane whispered, "Maybe you'd better let Lucy Blair play it — "

"I'm the director of this troupe, Jane. I'll assign the parts, if you don't mind."

"I'm sorry."

Angus stood up, and flung the script on the table.

"Maybe you're too tense, trying too hard. We'll do another scene this afternoon, and you can take the afternoon off. Go somewhere quiet and dig into that scene and see if you can't come up with something a little less like the monthly programme of the Ladies' Aid and Comfort Society."

His voice had stung on the last words. He turned and stalked out of the theatre. Jane put her head down on the kitchen table around which they had been reading the play, and cried hard.

She had no idea how long she had been there alone, when a warm, friendly voice said above her, "Oh, come now; nothing can be as bad as that."

She jumped to her feet, glanced up at Mason Lawrence and then away.

"Is — are the others coming back?" she stammered.

"No, they're still lolling over a final cup of coffee and another cigarette," Mason answered her, smiling and friendly. "I missed you at lunch and came to see what was holding you up."

"I'm not hungry," she stammered again, unable to control her voice above the tears that clogged her throat.

"Andy been giving you a rough time?" Mason's voice was quiet and friendly. "Well, look, Honey, this season means an awful lot to him. The opening week will set the pattern for the whole season. If the show is good the first week, then we've got a chance. Andy's got every kopek in his bank-roll sunk in this thing; if it's a flop — well, Andy's going to be hunting a job, and that's going to be pretty bitter for a fellow like Andy."

"I know that, Mr. Lawrence — "

"I resent that!"

She blinked, startled out of her misery.

"Resent what?"

"Your addressing me as Mr. Lawrence. What are you trying to do, put me in an age group with Carlton James?"

A trace of color came into her tear-stained face, and she managed a slight smile.

"Of course not. It's just that — well, I'm shy, I suppose, and very much in awe of you — "

Mason's eyebrows went up and it was his turn to be startled.

"By the beard of the Immortal Bard!" he gasped. "In awe of *me?* I'm afraid to ask you why."

"Because you're such a wonderful actor. You're so at ease, so completely at home. It's — well, when you come on stage, you *are* the character; you're not just acting a part. I think you're wonderful!"

Mason eyed her for a long, startled moment, and then he gave a low whistle.

"To think that after all these years, an infant with sapphire-colored eyes and silver-gilt hair should say a thing like that to me!" he marveled.

Jane was very much in earnest.

"It's true, Mr. — I mean Mason!" she assured him. "I think I've seen you in every play you've done in and around New York. I've seen you in a few plays that were not good and that didn't last. But I've never seen you give a poor performance."

"Well, bless the child!" said Mason, grinning. "I suppose your dear old nursie took you to see me when you were only a tot?"

"I took myself, thanks, from the time I was seventeen and studying at the Dramatic Institute. That was three years ago."

Mason studied her curiously.

"That makes you twenty now, about three years older than I would have dreamed," he said after a moment. "But it still makes you — well, it doesn't reduce *my* age any."

"You're thirty-eight," she told him. "The most interesting age of all for a man."

Mason's eyes widened.

"Well, blow the man down!" he murmured,

and there was a glint of laughter in his eyes. "There must be some object behind all this pretty foolery. What can I do for you, my child?"

"You can stop treating me like a three-year-old, and then you can excuse me, because I've been given the afternoon off to crawl into a hole somewhere and study the finer feeling of my two side bit."

She stood up, a slender, lovely thing in her dark sun-back dress, her silver-gilt head held high.

"I take it Andy was somewhat less than overjoyed with your rather wooden performance this morning," drawled Mason. And swiftly, before she could resent that, he added gently, "It was, you know. But that's because you were nervous and taut. I'm not in the afternoon's rehearsal, either. So what say we find ourselves a quiet spot, which shouldn't be hard at all up here in this wilderness, and maybe I can help you. That is, if you'll let me?"

Her eyes were stars now, and the color was soft in her lovely face.

"Oh, *would* you?" she breathed.

"Look, Honey, I'm not handing you the keys to the kingdoms of all the world. I'm just offering to cue you while you ground yourself in your part. Don't make such a production of it," he protested.

"But if you've got the afternoon off, surely there must be other things you'd rather do," she protested.

His laugh was honest and delighted.

"That's either the most infantile or the most subtle remark any pretty girl ever made," he teased, then tucked his hand under her arm and marched her across the stage and out into the meadow. "I've been curious about that line of willows ever since we came here. Looks like a nice, quiet spot, don't you think?"

Beneath the willows, on the bank of the busy, narrow, self-important little stream, they sat on a grassy hummock and Mason opened the script.

"First of all, let's see what *you* think of the girl you're pretending to be? What sort of person does she seem to you?" he began.

For an hour or more, they worked; Mason correcting her now and then, clarifying in her mind some facet of the character, until at last Jane stared at him in amazement.

"Why, Sylvia is a real person, isn't she? She's coming alive. I'm beginning to see her, to understand her," she burst out.

Mason smiled, folded the script and said, "That's what acting is, my dear; understanding the character, seeing her alive, knowing what she would do, how she would react to the given situation. You have to forget, while you're on stage, who *you* are and concentrate on who 'Sylvia' is."

Quickly they went through the scene, with Mason cueing her, and then he smiled and nodded his approval.

"Play it like that at rehearsal in the morning and Andy will throw his hat in the air and stand on his head for joy," he told her.

"I don't know how to thank you," she said humbly.

Mason studied her for a moment, and then he chuckled, the imp of laughter in his eyes again.

"Oh, we'll think of something," he drawled, and added, "You're really crazy about show business, aren't you?"

Jane's lovely face hardened and the sparkle went out of her eyes.

"I loathe it!"

He was startled as much by the bitterness in her voice as by the words themselves, and he stared at her as though he could not possibly believe he had heard her correctly.

"You're joking, of course," he said at last.

"I was never more serious in my life!"

"Then why, in the name of heaven, are you battling to become an actress?"

"Because it's what my mother wants me to do."

Mason swore furiously.

"Now that's the craziest excuse I've ever heard in my life. You're twenty and you're *that* tied to your mother's apron strings? Oh, come now, Janie — leave us be sensible!"

"I know," Jane nodded, her face touched with bitterness. "It does sound silly. But it's what my mother has had her heart set on almost since the day I was born. When I heard about this chance to be an apprentice to Angus MacDonnell, Mother and Dad insisted on scraping up the tuition money and sending me money to live on because they are so sure that after this season as an apprentice to him, New York and Hollywood will be dangling fabulous offers in front of me."

Mason said, "And you don't agree with them? Your parents, I mean."

Jane met his eyes straightly.

"Do you?" she demanded.

Mason hesitated, and then he said quite honestly, "Frankly, Honey, unless you want terribly to be a good actress, and are willing to fight like the devil for every tiny chance, then you'd be a very smart child to do what *you* want to do — which is, I wonder, what?"

"Get married and raise a family," Jane told him.

Mason sat erect, staring at her.

"Well, for Pete's sake, why don't you do it then?" he wanted to know.

Jane smiled. "It takes two to get married," she pointed out.

"Don't tell me you haven't a long waiting list of eligible beaus clamoring for your hand?" His tone was teasing but the look in his eyes was warm and friendly.

"What chance would I have to meet young men who want to get married and raise families? Remember, I've been mixed up with other young people in my same field — only I seem to be the only one of them who isn't completely crazy about show business. But can you imagine one of the ambitious young men I meet at agents' offices, at the school, and here wanting to saddle himself with the burden of a wife and family?"

"I suppose not. After all, Kipling knew a thing or two when he made the statement that 'he travels fastest, who travels alone,' and in this business it's painfully true," admitted Mason, and jerked a thumb towards himself. "Exhibit A, who didn't get very far even if he did travel alone."

She looked at him for a long moment and

then she asked gently, "Have you minded so very much — being alone, I mean?"

He looked up at her quickly.

"What you really mean is, have I given up anybody I could have loved in order to pursue my alleged career? Frankly, no!" he admitted. "Matter of fact, to me show business is a job, not the end-all and be-all of a man's existence. Oh, sure, I enjoy it. It's a living; I'm enough of a ham to get a certain kick out of it. I suppose I'll knock around in it until I'm James' age, and then retire to a home for aged actors and bore the daylights out of anybody who will listen, showing off my scrapbook."

He chuckled and lowered his voice. "Want to know something? I don't even keep a scrapbook!"

She looked properly shocked. "I do," she told him quickly, and colored at his quizzical glance. "Oh, not about myself — how could I? I've never had any clippings to keep. But I keep one about you."

Mason was obviously startled and not too happily so.

"Why, you absurd creature, why should you?" he demanded at last.

She met his eyes straightly, though the color was high in her face.

"Because I've always admired you and have

always liked your plays, and why shouldn't I?"

"Because an infant like you should be collecting pictures of stalwart young heros like — oh, like Farley Granger and Montgomery Clift and such — not an old war-horse like me!"

"You promised to stop treating me like a three-year-old," she protested. "I'll show you the scrapbook if you like. It's a very nice one, but I may not have *all* your clippings."

Mason laughed wryly.

"If you have more than half a dozen, I'm sure that's all," he derided, and stood up, holding out his hand to her. "Come on; let's get down to the village and change clothes and drive to Atlanta for dinner."

"Will Angus mind?" she asked.

He smiled. "Oh, I know he keeps a pretty tight rein on the apprentices, but I'm sure he'll be agreeable as long as he is quite sure we'll both be on deck in the morning at nine. Which we will be, I promise."

As they passed the theatre going toward the waiting cars, they could hear the rehearsal going full power, and Mason winked at Jane, who giggled as they pretended to sneak to the car and away.

Chapter 9

On Saturday night before the opening of the season, the big barn had been decorated for the party Angus had known that it would be smart politics to give, so that both the mountain people and the summer visitors could become familiar with the entertainment scene he had planned for them. Wisely, he had engaged an orchestra made up of half a dozen mountain men, with Fiddlin' Bill, famous throughout the section for his calling of the beloved squaredances.

Ben, who came late, stood just inside the entrance, watching the scene, wide-eyed and amused, yet a little sorry about the transformation though he knew that he was wrong to feel so.

A woman beside him, in a crisp white pique sun-back frock that was almost as frontless as it was backless, stood on tiptoe to eye the orchestra and said laughingly to her friend, "I didn't know Spike Jones had taken to barn-storming."

Ben grinned dryly and moved away, looking for Lessie. But when he saw her she was dancing with Angus MacDonnell, and laughing as though having a marvelous time. He had been late, because he had had to go down to headquarters in the village, and there had been no reason she should wait for him. He had wanted her to have fun and it was obvious that she was. So there was no need for him to hang around here. He was tired and his mother was alone. So he turned and walked across the moon-silvered parking space to his car.

A couple was sitting in it, and as Ben approached it with long strides, there was a scramble, and the two were standing beside the car when he reached it. In the moonlight, the girl was radiantly lovely in a printed cotton frock. The man beside her was wearing a light sports jacket and lighter flannels.

"I'm so sorry — is this your car?" The girl's voice was soft and caressing. "Juddy and I simply could not take another moment of those *awful* hill-billies. Heavens, where do they come from? Such benighted creatures — "

"Oh, we manage to get along. We did even before we were invaded," said Ben.

Startled, he heard the girl gasp, "Oh, but surely *you're* not one of these — "

"Hill-billies? I'm happy to say I am, Miss — "

"I'm Elaine Harlowe — "

"Then if you'll excuse me, Miss Harlowe — " Ben indicated his car, and Elaine moved unwillingly from beside it and laid a swift, pleading hand on Ben's arm.

"I do hope I wasn't offensive, Mr. — ?"

"I'm Ben Logan."

"Then I do apologize, Ben, with all my heart! If you're one of the mountain people, then I've misjudged them." Elaine's voice was warm and winning.

"I'm afraid it won't matter greatly to the people up here what you think of them one way or another, Miss Marlowe, any more than it would matter to the mountains that you didn't like them. They and their people have been here for a good many years, and I daresay they'll last a few more."

Ben got into his car and drove away, and Jud and Elaine stood looking after the car. Jud whistled under his breath and looked accusingly down at Elaine.

"Now you've really pulled a boner," he told her. "You know how hipped Angus is on 'good public relations.' When he finds out you've snooted one of the most prominent citizens in these parts, he's going to be good and sore. In case you don't know it, the gent you've just met is engaged to our charming landlady, the Howell girl."

"Engaged? That handsome creature to that sappy little dame? Oh, Juddy, that's terrible."

Jud frowned at her, uneasy and disapproving.

"What's terrible about it? They both belong here; we're what he called us: invaders. They've lived here all their lives — "

"And that's probably why he thinks he's in love with her," Elaine mused.

"Thinks he's in love with her?"

"Oh, but he couldn't be, not really. She's — well, she's such a dopey creature. She actually enjoys cooking and messing around with house-keeping. Why, Jud, would you believe it if I told you she actually does the laundry? I've seen her hanging the most terrific mass of freshly washed clothes on the line."

Jud studied her in the clear moonlight, and what he saw in her lovely face he did not like at all. Some of the fascination and the spell-binding glamour he had found in her faded into nothingness. Her full, lipsticked mouth held a faint smile that was faintly cruel; her eyes were slightly narrowed. She looked, thought Jud suddenly, like a big, sleek cat with designs on a small, unwary rabbit.

Elaine caught the harshness in his voice

and tilted her head to look up at him, cool-eyed and remote.

"So?" She tinged her voice with derision.

"Look, Elaine," his voice was harsh, "I have no intention of getting myself fired before the season opens. Whatever you're cooking up in that devious mind of yours, I want no part of it. These people have been kind and friendly; and for you to go around flinging the word hill-billies in their faces is very bad manners and darned poor public relations. Get yourself fired if you want to — "

Her gay trill of laughter was like a hand laid on his lips, silencing him.

"Angus MacDonnell fire me?" She seemed to find the thought terribly amusing. "You'd come closer to the facts if you said I might fire him."

Jud felt like slapping her. "Oh, yeah?" He was deliberately rude. "And who are you, if I may make so bold as to ask?"

"Why, I'm the girl who's responsible for half his bank-roll, and there's a drawing account for more if he needs it. If he fires *me*, the season is over," Elaine drawled.

Jud was unpleasantly startled and frankly skeptical.

"You mean you're backing the show? Financing the season? I don't believe it!"

"Oh, not out of my own funds, naturally." Elaine was lightly amused at his bewilderment. "But my producing company is. The Paragon Productions, Inc., of Hollywood and wherever, who signed me to a contract after a test they liked. They wanted me to have more experience, some that I couldn't get just by attending their drama school on the coast. So I was farmed out to MacDonnell for this season in summer stock. I'm to be 'groomed for stardom' as it says in the movie-magazines; and in consideration of that, Paragon Pictures is underwriting the season here, as much as MacDonnell will accept. He was short of funds and wanted some really good plays to produce, and the royalty demands were beyond him. So Paragon is providing the plays, and whatever else MacDonnell needs. Him fire me? Juddy, darling, don't make me laugh."

Jud looked down at her, brushing her hand from his arm as though he had found the touch distasteful.

"So you were lying," he accused.

"I wasn't, Juddy. It's the truth. Only — well, I wasn't supposed to tell anybody. It was supposed to be a secret, so Teresa wouldn't blow her top and walk out on the show. As long as she feels I'm just a member of the company, playing second leads and all that, and that she outranks me, everything will be fine. But if she finds that I'm being backed by Paragon, and that Angus Mac-Donnell can't fire me — "

"Oh, be quiet!" snapped Jud sharply. "Don't ever think for a minute he couldn't fire you, or that he wouldn't, if you stepped out of line."

"Darling, don't be cross," she pleaded coaxingly, swaying closer to him so that the heady, exotic scent she wore could reach up to him and make him aware of her as an exciting, alluring woman. "I shouldn't have offended the Howell girl's boy-friend. I'll make amends first chance I get. And I shouldn't have told you about Paragon Pictures and all the rest of it. I didn't mean to, Juddy — honestly, it just slipped out. I loathe it down here! And I'm so darned lonely; no one has been even civil to me except you! Don't *you* get mad at me, Juddy — please!"

She slid an arm about him, her hand caressing the back of his head, drawing his face down to hers as she gave him a warm, lingering kiss.

Jud accepted the kiss then returned it. His arms drew her close, and his voice was husky.

"You're a very dangerous woman, Elaine, my dear. Very, very dangerous, and I'm a fool to listen to you — "

Elaine's chuckle was like the soft purring of a contented cat.

"Of course I'm dangerous, darling. Every woman is, given the right man and the right setting," she cooed. And then with a thread of anxiety in her sweet, caressing voice, she asked, "You *do* promise not to tell, Juddy darling?"

"I won't tell as long as you behave yourself," said Jud, holding her tightly. "But one false move, and you'll have yourself to blame for what happens."

Elaine laughed softly, and held up her mouth for his kiss. The moonlight did not show him the derision in her eyes, and his delight in her sweetness made his head swim a little.

Chapter 10

The dress rehearsal, the morning of opening day, had gone with the usual smoothness, occasionally interrupted as was inevitable by unforeseen difficulties. But when the curtain fell on the final act, Angus smiled at the cast and raised his clasped hands above his head in a victory gesture.

"Swell, kids! That was good. Do it just that way tonight and we're in. Take the afternoon off and catch your breath," he told them. And then to Jane, "Just a minute, Jane."

Jane caught her breath and looked up at Mason, who was beside her. Mason smiled encouragement and murmured, "Chin up, Honey. You were fine."

When the others had gone, Angus perched on the arm of the big sofa that occupied the space where the kitchen table had been during rehearsals and nodded at her.

"That was a very good performance you gave, Jane," he relieved the anxiety in her eyes. "I've been watching you during the last few days and I've seen a steady improvement. I just wanted to tell you how pleased I am."

Jane glowed with happiness.

"Mason will be so pleased," she said impulsively.

Angus looked puzzled.

"Mason? What's he got to do with it?"

"He's been helping me, coaching me. He's wonderful, isn't he?" Jane said joyously.

Angus studied her sharply, but his voice was light.

"Oh, Mason's quite a fellow. Only trouble with him is lack of ambition," he answered.

Jane flared indignantly, "Why, what a terrible thing to say! He *is* ambitious. He's a very fine actor. What's more, he's a very fine man!"

"Do you know what he wants more than anything else in the world, Jane?"

"Of course not," Jane's head was high. "Are you sure *you* do?"

Slightly nettled, Angus said, "Mason and I have been very good friends for many years. We probably know more about each other than you can imagine. Mason's chief ambition is to get enough money together to retire to some small town, and spend the rest of his life puttering around. Living like a human being, he calls it."

"And what's so terribly wrong about that?"

demanded Jane, more than a trace of belligerence in her voice.

"Nothing, of course. Only it seems a terrible waste of the really great talent that he has."

"Perhaps he feels it's more important to be happy and contented than it is to be a great star. Maybe that's his ambition."

"I suppose so," Angus was tiring of the argument, and a little appalled to realize how deeply the girl was apparently involved with Mason Lawrence. "See here, Jane, when I took you on as an apprentice I promised to look after you; see that you didn't get into trouble — "

"I'm perfectly capable of looking after myself and I'm in no danger of getting into trouble," Jane assured him hotly.

For the moment she had forgotten that he was Angus MacDonnell, and that she was merely one of the humblest of his apprentices.

There was a momentary silence, and then she tilted her pretty chin and asked with icy politeness, "Will that be all, Mr. MacDonnell?"

Angus nodded. "That will be all, Jane — for the present."

She turned and walked off stage and out into the sun-drenched parking lot. Angus, still perching on the sofa arm, saw her get into the car with Mason, who had been waiting for her, and drive away.

Thoughtful, not too happy, Angus left the theatre, crossed the road and went up the lane to the Howell place where Caro and Teresa were helping Lessie get dinner on the big table out under the trees.

Angus looked swiftly around the group. Jud and Elaine were not present.

Teresa watched him, and when the meal was finished, she stood up and patted his shoulder.

"Come for a little walk, darling. I want to talk to you," she said gently.

Angus stood up, and with the eyes of the others upon them, they walked along the path through the orchard and up toward the spot where Teresa had first met Ellie. There she turned, smiled at him and dropped down on the springy, spicy carpet of pine needles and patted the ground beside her.

"Now, tell Mommie," she urged gently, tender raillery in her eyes. "What's bothering you? It can't be the play; it's going to be wonderful. Even the fair Elaine is behaving herself, and that's worth noting! So what is it?"

Angus smiled at her. "Am I that transparent?"

"Of course, darling. All men are, to the women who love them," she said serenely, and her smile warmed. "I *do* love you, Andy darling — you know how much and in what way! So I can say it without shame."

"I'm grateful," said Angus with an utter sincerity that made it a deeply moving phrase for all its brevity. "I'm a little worried about Jane, I admit."

"The Ellerbe child? Why, Andy, she's doing a beautiful job!"

"Guess who taught her how to play it?"

"Didn't you?"

Angus shook his head.

"Then who?"

"Mason Lawrence."

Puzzled, Teresa frowned.

"What's wrong with that? Next to you, I can't think of anybody more qualified to teach her — "

"And now she's in love with him."

"Oh, Andy, darling, don't be silly! Why, she's only a baby. He must be twice her age. She's got a school-girl crush on him, perhaps. Why, it will be years before she knows what being in love means — "

"She's twenty, Teresa."

Teresa studied him, a tender smile touching her mouth, a twinkle in her eyes.

"And Mason is what? Forty-ish?"

"Oh, somewhere between thirty-five and forty. What's that got to do with it? He's a darned attractive guy, one of the best — "

"Then where's the worry?"

"Jane's such a sweet kid. I don't want her hurt."

Teresa laughed and hugged him.

"Oh, Andy, darling, you can't carry the world on your shoulders! Jane will be in love and out of love a dozen times before she's thirty — and why not? How else can she learn to be a fine actress except by experiencing emotion?"

Angus looked down at her for a moment, and then he nodded and agreed, "Well, you're a woman *and* a fine actress. You should know."

The tender laughter vanished from Teresa's face and she looked down, pleating a fold of her skirt as though her whole mind were centered on the tiny task.

"Yes, I know." Her voice was unsteady. Then she looked up at him and said quietly, "I can never thank you enough, Andy, for what you are doing for me."

"You've got that wrong, Teresa. It's I who can never thank you for what you're doing for me, making the season a bowling success," he told her gravely.

"Oh, darling, don't say that! Never, never,

99

never even dare to think a show is a success until after the opening night and the reviews are in," she mocked him, but there was more than a trace of earnestness in her voice. "But you have got a good company, darling, and the line-up of plays is top-drawer. I find myself even beginning to like Elaine — well, I won't go quite that far. Let's just say I don't hate her as desperately as I did in the beginning, especially now that I know she's just on loan from Paragon Pictures."

Angus gave her a startled glance.

"Now, how did you discover that?" he demanded. "It's supposed to be a deep dark secret."

Teresa laughed. "A deep dark secret? With Elaine scattering broad hints all over the place? And besides, I read it in one of the gossip columns of a New York paper. Did you really think I'd mind, darling? That I'd be that petty and nasty?"

"There's no reason why you should mind. It was the others I was thinking about: how they would react to knowing that Elaine isn't really an apprentice, and that she will go straight to Hollywood when the season closes here. I felt it would make for better relations all around if they thought she was on an equal footing with them."

Teresa nodded thoughtfully.

"She's a very beautiful girl and probably screens like a million," she said. "What I can't understand is why Paragon Pictures wants her to be taught to act. The way she looks, the cash customers at the box-office ought to line up in droves just to look at her."

"Could be, only her company feels she has the makin's of an actress."

"And do *you* think so?"

Angus hesitated. "If ever she learns to take directions, and to behave herself and work hard, it's barely possible."

"Well, if she has it in her, you'll beat it out of her because you're one of the best," Teresa assured him, and then she slid her hand in his and said eagerly, "Andy darling, let's do a play on Broadway next season."

Angus said sharply, "Teresa, do you mean that?"

Teresa nodded. "I never meant anything more. I don't like my life much the way it was before you dragged me back to work, practically by the hair of my head. The days were endless; the nights were horrible. Now that I get up every morning with the knowledge that I have work to do, I'm tired enough at night when the curtain comes down to be able to sleep. I feel Ted would want it like that, don't you, Andy?"

Angus' hand covered hers where it lay on his arm and held it tightly.

"I know he would, Teresa dear. Talent like yours mustn't be wasted; all the years of hard work can't be thrown into the scrap-heap just because you have lost your taste for living. We'll do a play this fall; I'll wire Bill to start looking for a script for us," he told her eagerly.

She smiled at him warmly, her eyes misty.

"Dear Andy!" Her voice shook slightly. "What would I ever do without you?"

"I hope with all my heart you'll never have to find that out, Teresa. I hope to be on hand any time you need me, or want me around," said Angus. And there was a tone in his voice that made her look at him swiftly, and then away, while small fans of carnation-pink touched her face.

To break the brief tension Angus said in an entirely different tone, "And now what are we going to do about Jane and Mason?"

Startled, Teresa answered swiftly, "Nothing, of course. You can't meddle in people's lives, Andy. You're not *that* responsible for her, or for anyone else. You're behaving like a mother-hen with one chick. Andy, I have to ask you something. Smack me if you want to — but after all, Jane is a lovely thing. You're not — well, let's say just a wee mite jealous?"

Puzzled, he stared at her, frowning.

"Jealous?" he repeated, unable to follow her thought.

"All right, I'll put it brutally. Are you maybe interested in Jane?"

"Well, of course I am — as I am in all my people."

"Don't play stupid, darling, because that you aren't and couldn't ever be. I'm asking if you are a tiny bit in love with Jane yourself?"

Angus stared at her until he was sure she was in earnest, and then while the color poured into his face, he tipped his head back and laughed so heartily that a spark lit in Teresa's eyes.

"Well, after all, it's not that funny!" she snapped.

"Coming from you, it is," Angus assured her. "You, of all people, Teresa!"

Again there was that tone in his voice that brought color into her face, and her eyes were unable to meet his. There was a strange, unaccustomed shyness spreading through her, as though she had been Jane's age. With a sudden unexpected movement she stood up and turned away from him, starting back down the path. And after a moment, his eyes warm and tender, Angus followed her.

Chapter 11

Mrs. Logan stood, a tall, erect figure on the wide, old-fashioned porch, as she heard the sound of the car in the road. Loss of sight had quickened her sense of hearing until, no matter how many cars might pass, she could always recognize the sound of Ben's. She turned her sightless eyes toward the road, and though it had been many years since she had been able to see the scene before her, she knew every inch of it.

The car stopped and her keen ears caught the sound of voices, and she went down the steps and along the path to the car, hospitably greeting her visitor.

"Well, now, Lessie, it's mighty good to see you," she said, and was beautifully unconscious of the word. "I hear you've been right busy all summer."

"You know I must have been, Aunt Nancy, not to get over to visit with you more often." Lessie put her arm about the old woman's spare body as they turned back to the steps. Involuntarily, she put her hand under the elbow to guide Mrs. Logan up the steps.

Mrs. Logan jerked back and her white head went up.

"I can manage," she said curtly.

"I'm sorry — ." Lessie flung Ben an apologetic glance.

"Come along inside and have a glass of cider," said Mrs. Logan, and went up the steps and across the porch and into the house.

"Oh, Ben, I'm such a fool!" Lessie mourned. "I always forget that she loathes anyone trying to help her. She is so amazing I just can't seem to realize how independent she is."

"Don't worry about it, Honey. She's the same way with me when I try to take over any of the chores. Even weeding her flower garden is something she insists on doing herself," Ben soothed her tenderly.

They heard Mrs. Logan's businesslike footsteps, moving as briskly as though her eyes were as clear as their own, coming along the hall. She pushed open the door, carrying a heavy tray on which there was a tall, frosted pitcher with glasses beside it and a plate of cookies.

Ben made a move to take the tray but caught himself in time. His mother moved purposefully to the small table beside an old wooden rocker and put the tray down precisely in the center. And while they watched, fascinated, she poured three glasses full to the brim without wasting a drop and turned.

"I hear you've been mighty busy with them show-folks, Lessie," Mrs. Logan said. "Maggie Westbrooks says it's purely a sight what's been done to Grandsir Howell's barn."

"I'm afraid you wouldn't approve, Aunt Nancy, but after all the money will be very welcome when winter comes," Lessie answered.

"Well, I reckon Grandsir would be pleased and proud that he'd been able to leave something his folks could live on," Mrs. Logan agreed slowly, as though reluctant to admit it. "Reckon they'll be leaving soon, won't they?"

"In about six weeks," said Lessie. "I wish you could meet them, Aunt Nancy. They are very nice people, aren't they, Ben?"

"Some of them," Ben admitted cautiously.

"Ben, can't you find something to do with yourself for a while, and leave Lessie and me to talk woman-talk?" said Mrs. Logan suddenly.

Startled, Ben and Lessie exchanged a swift glance, and Ben stood up.

"I suppose so," he admitted. "Is there anything you'd like me to do for you? Some of the evening chores?"

Mrs. Logan lifted her face so that the sunlight fell on it, and smiled.

"It can't be more than three o'clock, and if you tried to milk Old Bessie this early in the afternoon, she'd kick you good and hard," she reminded him dryly. "Just go take a walk for yourself. Lessie will be perfectly safe with me."

"I never for a moment thought she wouldn't be," Ben said, his voice grim, as he walked away.

Mrs. Logan sat perfectly still, until the sound of his footsteps had died away. And then she turned her face toward Lessie, and Lessie had the absurd feeling that the old woman could see her clearly.

"There was a letter from Delsie two-three days ago," she said quietly.

"Would you like me to read it to you?" suggested Lessie, puzzled.

"Maggie read it to me when it came; she was spending the day with me. We were doing some canning and preserving, and I promised Ben I wouldn't do it when I was here by myself," explained Mrs. Logan, and went on heavily, "He doesn't know about the letter. I'd rather he didn't for a while. I don't know quite how I'm going to tell him, for he's going to take it mighty hard."

"Has something happened to Delsie? She's

sick — " There was quick alarm in Lessie's voice.

"Something's happened to her, but she ain't sick. She's married."

Lessie caught her breath from the shock and sat very still.

Mrs. Logan nodded as though she could read the shock on Lessie's face.

"She's not coming home this fall," Mrs. Logan went on heavily. "She's married her a fellow that's got a job in Alaska and she's already on her way out there with him. Of course, Delsie's mine same as Ben is, and she seems like she's real happy, or would be if she didn't feel she was sort of deserting Ben and me. Seems like she's mighty much in love with this feller, and he's got a good job and can take real good care of her. I'm proud that she's happy; but I'm mightly low-spirited at what this does to you and Ben."

Lessie could not answer. Among the dust and rubble of her bright castles, she sat stricken, and after a little Mrs. Logan continued.

"Maggie was right upset when she read the letter, so upset she gave me a good tongue-lashing — "

"She had no right to do that — "

"Seems she felt like she had, pointing out to me how I'm standing between you and

Ben, and you can't get married like you want to because I'm here and I got to stay here. It's not like I had much to want to go on living for, Lessie. If it was my choice, I'd quit right now — "

"Aunt Nancy, you mustn't say that!"

"I don't know how come I'm still here, a useless, no-'count old woman like me that's lived a lifetime, but I reckon my Lord and Master has some kind of a plan for me, and when He's ready for me to go, He'll send for me. And until He does, I wouldn't do nothing to speed my going — "

"Aunt Nancy, I won't listen to such talk — "

"You'll listen, Lessie. On account of I've wanted to say it a right long time and seems like I couldn't ever get the chance. I got it now, and you *got* to listen." Mrs. Logan was almost terrifying in her stern determination to have her way. "Maggie said I was a selfish, self-centered old fool not to be willing to pull up stakes and go live with you and Ben and the young-'uns at the Howell place, because there was plenty of room for me and you'd make me feel like I was welcome — "

"You would be, Aunt Nancy. You know you would be, always!"

Mrs. Logan's head went up and there was fire in her voice.

"I'm not even *about* to go somewheres where somebody would have to lead me around by the hand — where I'd have to be waited on. I'd sooner die!"

Appalled, Lessie could only sit silent, not daring to speak, afraid to protest, sickened by the anguish in the old woman's voice.

"I reckon that's what you and Ben are going to have to wait for," said Mrs. Logan at last. "For me to die."

"Oh, Aunt Nancy, how can you talk like that?"

"Reckon it's time the truth come out, Lessie. Way I look at it, you and Ben haven't got much chance as long as I'm living. There's no room here for you and your young-'uns. And there wouldn't never be room for me under another woman's roof, not even if there was forty rooms and only Ben and his wife there."

Lessie said quietly, "You hate me, don't you, Mrs. Logan?" And for the first time she found it impossible to use the courtesy term of "aunt" that is traditional among the mountain-folk for an older woman.

Mrs. Logan hesitated a moment and then she sighed.

"Reckon I don't hate you no more than any mother hates the girl that wants to marry her son," she said at last. "I don't just to say *hate* you, Lessie. It's just that I don't want Ben to marry you."

"I'm afraid I'll have to ask you why, Mrs. Logan, what you have against me. All these years you've never seemed to mind, when you've known all along that Ben and I loved each other. Why have you waited until now to tell me this?" Lessie's voice was low but quite steady, though there was a deep and bitter hurt in it.

"I got nothing against you personal, Lessie," the tired old voice said flatly. "It's just I don't want Ben saddled with a whole family of young-'uns to raise and educate and be worried with."

Lessie flinched from that and her tanned face whitened.

"I'm glad you are being frank with me at last, Mrs. Logan," she said evenly.

"I figgered it was a time to be frank, Lessie, to let you know how I felt."

"Well, that you surely have," Lessie answered her tautly. "Does Ben know how you feel?"

"I haven't talked to him about it. Men are funny people; where the woman they think they're in love with is concerned, men can be blinder than any fool bat."

"I see. So you feel that you love Ben more than I do."

"Now, that's a crazy-fool thing to say. I birthed him, didn't I? I've took care of him all his life. What did you ever do for him?"

"Just loved him more than anything in all the world."

"So's you can saddle him with a pack of responsibilities that are none of his seeking?"

"So that, if once I'm convinced that Ben wants to be free of me, I'll let him go without a whimper."

Mrs. Logan turned her sightless eyes toward Lessie, and her wrinkled old brown face was touched with a startled wonder.

"You mean that? You ain't just talking to hear yourself talk?" she demanded.

"Of course I mean it."

"Then I'm right glad we had this talk. Once Ben's free of you, he can find some other girl that'll come to him with no family but the ones they raise themselves, and that's the way it ought to be for two young people just starting out in life."

"You're that sure Ben wants to be free of me?"

"Oh, I reckon he don't think so now. Ever since you and him was tadpole size, you been courtin'. He never had much time even to look at another girl — "

"I was away at school at Laceyville, and Ben was overseas. That should have given him ample time to decide he didn't want me — "

"You come home ever' Friday and stayed till Sunday night, and he was with you most of the time. And while he was out yonder fightin', I reckon there wasn't many girls a fellow like Ben would be likely to notice much, even if he'd had time. And I reckon from what he says, he didn't."

Lessie heard Ben whistling as he came along the path. Swiftly she laid her hand on Mrs. Logan's, with a silencing gesture.

"We are the two women Ben loves best," she said softly, urgently. "We neither of us want to hurt him. We mustn't let him know that you feel as you do. Not yet."

"He'll have to know about Delsie getting married and not coming home."

"Will you let *me* tell him?"

"Reckon I'd be glad to. I don't relish the job none."

"Well, what have you two been cooking up against the race of men?" demanded Ben, as he came across the yard and to the steps.

"It's nothing that would interest you." Lessie made her voice very gay and mocking.

"You'd be surprised how interested I could be in anything that concerns my two best girls." Ben dropped a gentle hand on his mother's shoulder and smiled at Lessie. But as he caught the look she could not disguise in her eyes, his voice altered. "Don't tell me you two have been fighting?"

"Now, what would we have to fight about?" laughed Lessie, and stood up.

"Well, there's me," Ben pointed out, and the laughter had gone out of his voice.

"Such conceit! Aren't men silly? Let two women get their heads together and immediately a man is sure they're talking about him," said Lessie. "I really must be going. Good-bye, Mrs. Logan."

"Good-bye, Lessie." Mrs. Logan was politely formal, but force of habit made her follow the mountain custom of hospitality, and add, "You be comin' back again real soon."

"Thanks, I will," said Lessie, and ran down the steps and across to Ben's car.

"I won't be gone long, Mother," said Ben, and followed her.

As the sound of the car died away, Mrs. Logan folded her work-gnarled old hands and rocked gently, her face quite peaceful.

Chapter 12

As soon as the car had reached the highway, Ben pulled over beneath the shade of a friendly oak and turned to Lessie, his face stern.

"All right, let's have it. What did you and Mother quarrel about? And don't tell me you didn't, because I know both of you too well to be put off with any lies."

Lessie sat very still, her hands tightly locked in her lap, her face turned away from him so that he would not see the tears that filled her eyes.

"Delsie isn't coming home, Ben. She's married and gone to Alaska to live."

For a stunned moment, Ben sat staring at her, unable, even unwilling, to take in the full force of what she was saying.

"Delsie — " he began, and then roughly, "She couldn't — she wouldn't do such a thing — "

"She has, and your mother is delighted." Lessie's voice shook. "Because now you and I can't be married. And she's never wanted us to."

"Darling, you're out of your mind! Why, Mother is crazy about you. Oh, I know she doesn't make much of a display of her feelings — "

"She did today," Lessie reminded him. "She made it very plain that she has been opposed to our marriage from the very beginning."

"But, Lessie, that's crazy. Why *would* she be?"

"Because of the children." Lessie's voice broke, and Ben gathered her into his arms and held her closely, his scowling face against her soft, shining hair.

"Lessie, Lessie, don't cry, Honey — "

Lessie drew a hard breath and pulled herself from his arms.

"She's right, Ben, I guess. It wouldn't be fair for you to have to shoulder such responsibilities — they're not yours, but mine — "

"Lessie, we've been all over this a thousand times." Ben's voice was harsh. "You know I'm crazy about the kids; they like me; you need me to help you bring them up — "

"I need you just to love, and to love me!" stammered Lessie. "But your mother — Ben, she hates me. She wants you at home with her. She said we'd have to wait until she died. Oh, Ben, it was horrible, the things she said, sitting there rocking, looking at me as though she could see me and sort of gloating — "

"And all these years she has seemed pleased about us!" Ben was puzzled and deeply hurt.

"Because she didn't think there was much chance that we could go through with our plans. She was counting on something like this. She said if I really loved you, I'd set you free. Well, Ben, I *do* love you, and I am setting you free."

"Thanks," said Ben dryly. "Very kind of you, I'm sure. But it takes two for a deal like that, and I'm not playing."

Lessie turned her tear-wet face to his, and her smile was tremulous and unconvincing.

"This is terrible of me," she stammered. "I told her just now that she and I were the two women you loved most and that neither of us would willingly hurt you, yet here I am spilling all this. We are tearing you apart, between us. Ben, I didn't want it to be like this — oh, I didn't, I didn't — "

"Hush, darling, hush!" Ben soothed her at last to a broken sobbing that finally silenced itself against his shoulder. "I'll talk to her when I go home tonight. We've got to persuade her to — well, to be reasonable."

He took her home at last, and they could only look at each other, for neither had words for the parting. Lessie stood on the porch watching him as he went down the lane, and when she turned at last to go into the house her shoulders drooped and there was a defeated air about her that she was powerless to combat.

Chapter 13

It was cool and shady on the wide back porch, and Caro drew a deep breath as she came up the steps and sat down beside Lessie, who was shelling peas for tomorrow's lunch.

"Now about an extra hand?" she suggested cheerfully, and lifted a big pan of the peas and began shelling them. "You're worn out, Lessie. Don't you want Teresa and me to move out? And the cast to go jump in the lake, maybe? Now that the hotel coffee shop has opened down at the lake, there's really no point in your feeding a hungry horde of actors every noon, and putting up with Teresa and me — "

"I'd be lost if you were not here," said Lessie swiftly. "It helps me to keep busy."

"That it does, pal, that it does," Caro agreed, her eyes sharp on the girl's tired face. "But somehow, I have an idea that keeping busy is one of your smallest problems. I somehow can't imagine you sitting idle unless, say, between midnight and four A.M."

"You get used to it," said Lessie, trying to smile.

"I suppose." Caro's inexpert fingers with their glowing ruby-tipped nails spilled round green globules into the pan with a rattling sound, dropping the shells into a big pot between herself and Lessie. "I've heard you can get used to anything, even being hanged, if you just live long enough. I've never had any hankering to prove the old saying, though."

Lessie tried to laugh, but Caro continued to study her.

"I haven't seen the gorgeous hunk o' male around lately," said Caro, and the unexpectedness of it made Lessie catch her breath. "You haven't quarreled with him, have you?"

Color flowed into Lessie's cheeks as she said sharply, "Of course not."

"Good. You wouldn't want to leave valuable property around like that, unclaimed. There are too many predatory females on the prowl twenty-four hours a day," commented Caro, with her friendly grin. "When are you two planning to be married? I want to send you a gift — a humdinger — "

"We're not!" Lessie bit off the words, and Caro's eyebrows went up.

"Oh, I'm sorry. Me and my big mouth! I'm always talking out of turn. Only I thought everything was all set between you two."

"So did we," admitted Lessie, the need for a confidante loosening her tongue. "But his sister decided to marry someone who had a job in Alaska, and Ben can't leave his mother alone. She's blind and old."

"Old? How old?"

"Sixty-two."

"I resent that!" flashed Caro hotly. "Have you any idea how old I am?"

Lessie stared at her, puzzled.

"Forty, perhaps forty-five — " she stammered, puzzled by Caro's flash of temper.

Caro's grin was back. "Well, bless the child! Either you are the world's foremost liar or else you should be in the diplomatic service," she laughed, and looked around and lowered her voice. "Promise you'll keep my secret?"

"Of course." Lessie was puzzled.

"On my next birthday — and it's in October — I'll be fifty-seven, darn it," said Caro. Then she shrugged and added, "Oh, well, maybe I might as well tell the truth. I'll be sixty-one."

"I don't believe it!" gasped Lessie.

Caro bridled a little, even as she laughed.

"Well, bless you for that, but it's the truth. And you dare to sit there and call your boy-friend's mother old at sixty-two! Why, that's just the prime of life — I keep telling myself!"

"It's different with mountain people, who work hard from can't-see to can't-see," Lessie pointed out.

"Now there's a phrase I must add to my collection — as soon as you tell me what it means. 'Can't-see to can't-see.' Riddle it for me, Honey."

"Oh, it just means getting up while it's so dark you can't see, and working until it's so dark at night you can't see," laughed Lessie.

She went on shelling peas, and Caro watched her, tenderness and genuine affection in her eyes.

"So Mom doesn't want sonny-boy to get married," she mused at last. "Isn't it funny? Sometimes I wonder how any man ever gets married, if his mother is still living. Every mother believes the girl hasn't been born who is good enough for her son, even if Sonny is the lowest thing that ever crawled. I'd think any woman in her right mind would climb up on the rooftop and shout for joy at the prospect of having you for a daughter-in-law."

"It's the children," said Lessie painfully, awkwardly.

"The children?" Caro was puzzled.

"Mrs. Logan doesn't want Ben saddled with responsibilities. I suppose maybe any mother would feel that way." Lessie was very near tears, but there was relief in confiding some of her grief to this friendly, warm-hearted woman.

"From what I've seen of the children — and living here in the house this summer, I've seen plenty — they're as fine a bunch of kids as anybody could want to see around. The old girl must be balmy!" Caro protested hotly. "Anyway, your man's grown up, and surely not tied to her apron-strings."

"You don't understand. She's blind, and she and Ben live all alone, and there are no neighbors close at hand. He couldn't just walk out on her — and she won't come here."

"Nor let you bring your brood with you there?"

"There's no room there," answered Lessie quickly. "They have only a five room house. Even if there were fifteen rooms, I wouldn't take the children where they're not welcome."

"Well, of course you wouldn't! Judas! What an old battle-axe!"

"She isn't, really. She's a grand old lady, but she's — well, she's set in her ways, and because she has lived practically her whole life in that house, where nothing is ever moved, she can find her way around the place without any difficulty whatever. She keeps house, cooks, tends her garden and is as independent as though she had full sight. But here everything would be strange to her, and she would — well, there's no use talking about it. She told me she'd sooner die than leave her home and come here to live with us."

Caro asked curiously, "And the children are her only objection to your marrying her beloved son? Zounds, doesn't she realize that in a few years the children will be grown up and going their own way?"

Lessie nodded. "Oh, I suppose so. Jim will be going into the army in September and he's terribly excited about it. And Mary Sue wants to be married, but she's promised me she will wait until she is eighteen; she's sixteen now, almost. But there's Butch, and Ellie."

Inside the big old-fashioned kitchen, Mary Sue, wide-eyed and pale beneath her tan, crept on silent feet down the hall and out on to the front porch, where she stood for a moment trembling, clinging to the rough bark of the old porch pillar.

She drew a deep, hard breath and clenched her hands tightly. She had known that something was troubling Lessie, but she had thought it was merely the strain and physical weariness of a busy summer. She realized now that Ben hadn't been around in more than a week; she had been too absorbed in her own youthful affairs to pay much attention to the fact. But now, standing in the kitchen, hearing Lessie and Caro, it had come to her in a blinding, stunning blow. Lessie was being denied marriage with Ben because she, Jim, Butch and Ellie stood in the way.

She went down the steps and around the lane, keeping out of sight of the house, until she found Jim, chopping wood out beyond the barn.

Jim looked up and grinned, but his grin faded as he caught her pallid, wide-eyed look.

"What is it? Did you step on a snake?" he demanded, coming swiftly to meet her. "Did you kill it — "

Mary Sue clutched at him, and Jim put his arm around her, frowning because she was trembling.

"It wasn't a snake, Jim," she said, brushing aside his anxious query. "Look, Jim, did you know that Mrs. Logan won't let Ben marry Lessie because of us?"

Jim stared at her, thunderstruck.

"Well, what's the matter with us that she

don't like us?" he demanded.

"There's — there's too many of us," stammered Mary Sue, and tears spilled down her face and she clung to Jim. "Oh, Jim, we've got to figure some way of getting around Mrs. Logan."

"I'd like to get around her with a baseball bat! Sure, I know she's an old woman and blind as a bat, but that's no reason why she should make trouble for Lessie. Pete's sake, Ben's almost thirty. Why does he have to have his mother's consent?" Jim exploded.

"Oh, don't be silly. You know Ben couldn't go away and leave her there all alone, and she *won't* come here — "

"She'd better not!" Jim's voice was grim.

"Jim, what are we going to do? Lessie and Ben — why, golly, they've been in love with each other almost their whole lives! Delsie was supposed to get her training as a teacher and come home and stay with her mother. Only something's happened, I guess, and she's changed her mind. Anyway, Lessie's just about heart-broken. And it's all because of us."

"Well, I'm going into the army in September, when I pass my birthday," said Jim. "That will take one of us out of the way."

"I suppose I could go down to Laceyville,

or maybe to the lake and get a job and go to school — "

"That's out and you know it. Lessie wouldn't let you."

"Well, even if she did, that would still leave Butch and Ellie."

"I suppose the old witch thinks Lessie should stash us under a rock or something, or maybe drown us!" said Jim bitterly.

"Oh, Jim, what are we going to do?" Mary Sue wept.

"I don't know, chicken," Jim answered, patting her shoulder awkwardly. "But we'll think of something."

"We've got to, Jim, we've just got to!" said Mary Sue shakily.

"We will, kid, we will. I don't know what, but *something!*" Jim promised her. But there was not much conviction in his voice as he stared into the pale gray-lavender shadows of dusk that were creeping up the valley as the sun slid down behind Old Baldy's blue shoulders.

Chapter 14

Jane tossed back her shining hair, laughing joyously as the speedboat scampered across the dimpling blue waters, and Mason smiled at her.

"Having fun?" he asked unnecessarily.

"Oh, so much fun!" she gave the expected answer. "It's been such a wonderful summer, and only a month of it left! Isn't that awful?"

"Oh, well, New York is fun in the autumn — or I've heard so-called popular songs that say so."

Some of Jane's joyous gaiety vanished.

"Funny, the song-writers don't seem to know much about sitting for hours on hard benches in agents' offices and pretending gaily that you don't really need a job, that you are just in show business for the kicks. Even when you are starving, you have to pretend that everything is wonderful and that you're only pulling for the job because you've read the play and you feel the part you're asking for is so exactly right for you! And all the time everybody knows you're lying in your teeth and if you don't get the part, or another one that pays as well, you'll probably go on relief — if you can!"

"That's part of show business, Janie," Mason told her.

"Another part of it I don't like."

"Why not give it up then and go home and marry the boy next door and settle down and raise a family?"

"Probably because there isn't any boy next door, and because my mother is counting on me to realize all her ambitions."

They brought the speedboat into the dock and Mason helped her out. As they started back up to the motel cabins, he looked down at her.

"Well, after this season with Andy you shouldn't have too much trouble getting an agent to front for you," he suggested, and smiled tentatively.

"I have you to thank for the season here."

She looked up at him soberly and added, "I'm not too sure I'm grateful, either."

"Hi, what kind of talk is that? How could I be responsible for your staying on during the season?" he protested.

"By coaching me, helping me to get the proper interpretation of the part, of course," she answered quickly. "Andy said so. He's a little worried, by the way."

"Worried?" Mason was even more puzzled.

They had come to the row of motel cabins facing the lake now and had paused beneath the shade of an enormous oak. Jane stood looking out over the lake, her face turned away from him, and when she spoke her voice was so low, so quiet that for a full instant he scarcely took in the full meaning of her words.

"He's afraid I'm becoming emotionally involved," she said, and then she turned her head and looked straight into his eyes. "He thinks I'm falling in love with you."

Mason was startled, and his brows drew together.

"Oh, Andy wouldn't be such a fool — " he began, but her quiet voice went on, ignoring his protest.

"And of course he's right. I *am* in love with you. But you mustn't let it bother you. I know you'd never give me a second thought and that you've helped me only because you're such a perfectly wonderful person and because you're sorry for me. I shall always be in love with you, but you mustn't let that worry you. I'd rather be hopelessly in love with you than happily in love with anybody else in the whole wide world."

She took a step away from him, and Mason broke the paralysis of amazement and shock sufficiently to put out his hand and catch her by the arm, staying her, bringing her back to face him.

"Oh, no, you don't!" His voice was harsh. "You don't just toss a bombshell like that and then calmly walk away. This has got to be discussed — "

"There's nothing to discuss," she told him steadily, though there was a mist in her eyes. "I've said it, and that's all there is to say — "

"Not by a darned sight it isn't! Why, you little goof! You can't possibly be in love with me!"

"Can't I?"

"Of course not. Why, I'm old enough to be your father."

"That's silly. What's age got to do with it? You're everything any girl could want; you're handsome, attractive, you have great charm, sophistication — " Her voice shook and she set her teeth hard in her lower lip to control its trembling. "Please, I don't want to talk about it. You don't have to tell me what a fool I am; I know it. And I don't expect anything at all of you except I'd like it a lot if you'd go on being my friend."

She broke away from him then and went running down the path in front of the cabins until she reached the one she shared with Elaine. The door banged shut behind her even as Mason still stood, staring after her, badly shaken.

He had been so careful not to reveal his true feeling for her. He had reminded himself over and over again that she was a child, a sweet, endearing, engaging child, and that she was grateful to him for what he had been able to do in getting her up in her parts, earning Andy's approval. But he had assured himself over and over again that nothing at all could come of their relationship.

But now the simple, straightforward confession she had made had shaken him badly. A door in his heart that he had very firmly shut and locked threatened to swing open. But he mustn't allow it to. Not to this child! Because to him she was a child. She would fall out of love with him as soon as the season was over and they were back in New York. This idyllic setting that had thrown them into such close contact had blinded her. Old devil propinquity had convinced her that she was in love with him. But it wasn't true. It couldn't be true! It — well, blast it, it mustn't be true!

He drew a deep, hard breath, lit a cigarette with a hand that shook very slightly, and strode off to the cabin he shared with James.

Carlton sat in one of the canvas beach

chairs in front of the cabin, a pile of theatrical magazines in his lap, *Variety* in his carefully manicured hand.

"Ah, there, my boy." Carlton was already in the spirit of his part in the week's shows, being very much the somewhat pompous man of affairs. "What have you been up to all afternoon? Haven't seen you since morning rehearsal."

"I rented a speedboat and took Jane for a spin," said Mason, and dropped into the chair beside Carlton's.

Carlton lowered *Variety* and looked over his horn-rimmed glasses at Mason, his eyes speculative.

"You're seeing quite a bit of the child, aren't you, m'boy?" he suggested, carefully careless.

Mason looked at him sharply.

"And what do you mean by that?" he snapped.

Carlton shrugged elaborately.

"Drop it," he said in his own tone of voice. "I see some friends of mine are doing very well in the Citronella Circuit around New England. It's going to be good to get back to Broadway. The country, rural scenery, the bucolic atmosphere is all very well for the summer, but I'll take Broadway any time."

"Or Hollywood?" suggested Mason dryly.

"There's no room for me in Hollywood. Character actors of my age and ability are a dime a dozen out there. It wounds my pride deeply to admit they're fairly common around Broadway, but — well I manage to eat and to keep up my membership in the Lambs," Carlton said with an unexpected frankness. "You're the type for Hollywood, m'boy, not me."

"Thanks," said Mason curtly.

"Oh, well, if you can stand having fantastic sums shaken in your face by Hollywood producers, and still turn them down — "

"Hollywood producers aren't exactly beating a path to my door, Carl. I'm too old for a leading man and not old enough yet for your kind of character parts," Mason reminded him.

"But exactly right for the smooth, sophisticated 'heavy' who uses his evil charm to lure the innocent maiden from the arms of her true love, Johnny Stalwart."

Mason frowned. "What brought this on, anyway?"

"I'm sure I wouldn't know," Carlton answered affably.

"You made some crack about my seeing a lot of Jane. What did you mean by that?" Mason's voice sounded taut and angry.

Carlton's white eyebrows went up and his

pink, well-barbered face had the innocence of a baby.

"A 'crack,' my dear boy? What a crude way to put it. I merely mentioned that you and Jane seemed to have, as the gossip columnists put it, 'found each other.' I assure you I meant nothing unpleasant. After all, living on top of each other as we always do in a stock company, it's difficult not to see rather more of each other than we sometimes like."

"I've been coaching her."

"Indeed you have, and her work is improving enormously. You're an excellent coach."

"And now the absurd infant thinks she is in love with me!" Mason burst out.

Carlton did not laugh. He merely nodded.

"So she finally told you, did she? The rest of us have known it since the opening week," he said frankly. "But don't let it get you down, m'boy. She'll get over it. It's a part of growing-up pains. A hopeless crush on an older man is an inevitable part of a girl's growing up."

Mason looked at him sharply.

"You think that's all it is?" he asked anxiously.

Carlton made a gesture with the hand that held *Variety*.

"My dear boy, what else could it be? You surely don't think it's serious? No more so than shipboard romances, the two-weeks-with-pay vacation kind?"

Mason was startled to realize that he did not care too much for the thought. He was unpleasantly conscious that he did not want Jane to forget him.

Carlton watched Mason from the corner of his eye and saw the mixed emotions registered in Mason's face. And even as he grinned slightly, and raised his magazine to shield his face, there was a wistful look of long-dead memories in his faded eyes.

Chapter 15

Mrs. Logan came back across the yard, moving with a sureness of step that bespoke her long familiarity with every inch of the place.

She had fed the chickens, and now she must get supper started, for Ben would be home soon. She sighed as she mounted the steps and put the basket of eggs carefully down on the bench beside the door.

Ben hadn't been like himself lately. It not only worried her, it disturbed her conscience, for she knew that she was the cause of the change in him; that he was grieving for Lessie because he couldn't marry her and that his mother stood between them.

"But there just ain't anything I can do about it, Lord," she whispered as she stood for a moment at the kitchen door, her face lifted to the sky.

She tied a clean gingham apron over her neat calico dress and struck a match, bending to light the fire Ben had laid in the wood-stove before he had left this morning. She'd cook him a good supper tonight; the things he liked best. And maybe he'd eat with more appetite than of late. In every way she could conceive she was trying to placate that voice that whispered within her; trying to tell it she would make amends for her wickedness. She would do *anything* — except give her consent to this marriage. That was the one thing she couldn't, wouldn't do! It was beyond her strength.

The big kerosene-oil lamp in the center of the table had to be lighted. It scared Ben when he came up the lane at night and the light wasn't on. For herself, of course, it didn't matter. It was always night to her and there was never any light, but for Ben's sake the lamp had to be lighted. So she took a long kitchen match from the box over the stove and, moving surely, lifted the globe from the lamp, touched the match to the wick, waited for it to ignite, and then, steadying it with her hand, started to fit the globe back in place.

What happened she afterwards could never quite decide. Perhaps, because she was worried and disturbed, her hand was less sure than usual. Instead of the globe fitting neatly in place, it missed, the lighted lamp tilted, and she heard it roll to the floor and break; instantly she felt the flash as the lighted wick met the spilled oil.

She staggered backward, and for a moment

panic touched her. Where was the door to the back porch? She had to get out! The house would roar up in flames; she couldn't put out the fire without seeing it. She could feel the heat, hearing the flames eat greedily into ancient wooden floor, leaping from chairs to wall. She gathered her crisply starched calico skirts around her, and gave a sob of relief as she assured herself that they were not on fire.

She stumbled backward, and in that moment of panic her accustomed assurance here in her own small cabin deserted her. Where was the door? And how could she be sure she was finding the right door, getting out of the house, not just running from room to room like a chicken with its head chopped off! She made a terrific effort to pull herself together, even as she jerked backward from the increasing heat and her hand found a door-knob and twisted it, and fresh, crisp night air flowed over her. She went stumbling, clinging to the porch railing, found the steps and got down them, and out into the back yard. But where to now? The woods were bone-dry, and the house was surrounded by ancient trees; the fire would spread and spread and she could be trapped almost as easily out of doors as in.

If only Ben would come! If only she could

find the lane down to the road. Sobbing, terrified as she had never been before in all her self-sufficient life, she went stumbling around, all her well-learned knowledge of the place wiped from her mind now in this sickening panic. She caromed off a huge tree, and stumbled back to it, clinging to it, listening to the increasing roar of the flames as they fed hungrily on ancient wood and furniture, leaping to the big trees outside.

If she could back to the field behind the barn — where there were no trees, nothing to burn. If she could find her way there and to the middle of the field, she'd be safe. If this big tree she was clinging to was at the back of the house, if she had come out of the back door, as she thought she had, then she had only to move due west away from the house and she'd find the field. But if this was the big tree beside the lane, then any attempt she might make to reach the highway would lead her through woods and trees that at any minute now would become flaming torches.

Oh, Lord, let me find the field. Dear Lord, let me find the field, she prayed, and heard a crashing sound that told her the roof of the house had collapsed.

There was no time to waste in thinking. There was only time to get away from that searing inferno whose heat was already reaching out toward her. She went stumbling, hands outstretched before her, across the clear space and came up hard against a wire fence, and sobbed with joy. The chicken fence! It had to be! If she could feel her way around the fence, it would lead her to the patch down behind the lot and to plowed field where she would be safe!

Sobbing in her panic and shock, she reached the corner of the chicken fence and went on. And then she paused, newly frightened. If she kept on, clinging to the fence, she would bring herself right back to the corner of the barn. And the house was so near it, with the big tall shade-trees she had always loved but which now were an added threat to her, that she would be back in danger again. It was hard to release her clutch on the post of the chicken fence when she felt she had reached the corner nearest the field. Her only safety, she knew, lay in reaching the middle of the plowed ground and crouching there until someone saw the fire and help came.

"Ben," she sobbed, "oh, Ben, Ben, forgive me, and come soon."

It was a prayer as devout as that she had addressed to the Deity, and there was some small measure of comfort, in her peril and panic, to realize that Ben would be on his way home now and that it would not be long until she would be rescued. *If she could reach the field!*

She stood still for a long moment, bracing herself to the fact that she must let go of the fence-post and give up its frail support, so that she might escape to the field. If only she was headed in the right direction. Fear clawed at her. Panic was something she had rarely known since her blindness. But now the familiar landmarks so long known to her had been wiped out by the panic that had sent her plunging so wildly out of the house.

She tried desperately to fight down the panic, to orient herself, but she had made so many turnings, had stumbled so out of her accustomed paths that it was impossible for her to grasp her usual sure-footed way. But because she could hear the roar of the flames behind her, even feel the heat of the fire against her sightless face, she knew she must give up her clinging to the post and go forward. With a prayer she moved forward a step, and then another, away from the fence, hearing the frightened squawking of the chickens, the lowing of Old Bessie, the cow, the wild grunting and squealing of the pigs, an undercurrent to the fury of the fire.

She took a step, and then another and another, her hands outflung against any obstacle that might be in her path. And then thankfully beneath her stumbling feet she felt the plowed ground and knew she had reached the field and that now she had only to keep stumbling on until she was far enough inside its area to be safe from the fire. And then she sank down, shaking, unable to move another step . . .

To Ben, driving home in the late afternoon, his heart heavy within him, the tell-tale glow in the sky was a spur that made him jam his foot harder on the accelerator. But it was not until he had rounded the shoulder of the mountain and could see ahead that his worst fear was realized. It was his own home that was burning! The flames leaped high, reaching hungrily for the beautiful old shade-trees, the cedars that lined the lane. Even as he turned in the alarm on the walkie-talkie set and raced up the lane, his heart was in his throat, his thoughts on his mother. This was the fear that had nagged at him all these years, but his mother had scoffed at such fears, had insisted on her cherished independence, her ability to take care of herself.

Overhead he could hear the helicopter, already sending its own message, assembling fire-fighting equipment, warning all the nearby residents by hovering above the fire, pinpointing it.

The next half-hour was a blur of horror to Ben, as other cars began to converge. People came from every direction to help a neighbor in peril, swift, efficient, but too late. The cabin was smoldering ruins; the age-old trees ruined and blasted.

They had saved the barn and the frightened chickens, the pigs and the cow. But Ben could only stand dazed and sick, looking at the smoldering ruins of the cabin, knowing that his mother must be somewhere in all that hideous mass of ruin.

He covered his face with his hands, and friends from the forest-station, neighbors, men who had known him all his life, stood awkwardly by, knowing the futility of words at such a moment.

There was a painful silence in which no one could speak. Then suddenly a man lifted his head, straining his ears, moving swiftly away from the group around Ben, and toward the back of the place.

The beam of his powerful flashlight made a path of light ahead of him, and he paused now and then to listen; reluctant to arouse in Ben a hope that might be doomed to destruction, yet feeling that he did hear, through the cool dusk, a voice lifted in a cry for help.

And so it was that he found her: a bundle of calico and gingham, face down in the plowed field, supporting herself on her scrawny, shaking arms, using the last of her fast ebbing strength to cry aloud for help.

"Ben?" she wailed, barely above a whisper, as she felt the light on her face, and gentle arms lifted her.

"No, ma'am, it ain't Ben; it's Bill Henshaw," said the man, one of the youngest of the rangers, her son's good friend, as he lifted her easily in his arms as though she had been a child. "Ben's here, though. Just don't you worry none. I'll take you to Ben."

He walked swiftly, untroubled by his frail burden, back around the chicken fence, and as he came within sound of the others, he gave a shout.

"Here she is, Ben. She's all right!"

There was a stunned moment of silence, and then a great shout went up and the group of men came hurrying toward Bill. There were unashamed tears on Ben's face as he gathered his mother into his arms and held her tightly.

"Are you all right, Mother? Oh, Mother — " His voice broke and he laid his cheek against hers for a moment. "Are you hurt?"

"Not hurt, just scared. Oh, Ben, it was so clumsy of me. I tilted the lamp while I was waiting for the wick to catch; trying to put the shade on. Oh, Ben, I was so scared!" She whimpered like a terrified child as she clung to him with shaking arms.

"Here, Ben, let me see." It was old Doctor Parmenter, their nearest neighbor. "Put her down here in the car and let me see if she got any burns."

Feebly Mrs. Logan struck his hands away.

"Don't you go pawing me, Doc. I tell you, I'm all right. I didn't get burned. I was just scared and run like a blind dog in a meat house, that's all. I'm all right now." Her shaking voice carried little of her usual force and authority, but Doctor Parmenter stepped back, grinning.

"Best get her to bed, Ben, and keep her there a few days, and she'll be all right," he said quietly.

"The hospital at Laceyville, don't you think?" suggested Ben anxiously.

"No!" There was a returning vigor in Mrs. Logan's voice. "I'm not going to no hospital."

"Be proud to have her at our house, Ben — "

Several voices chimed in, and then Mrs. Logan spoke, and her voice was abashed and humble, two qualities Ben could never remember hearing before in his indomitable old mother's voice.

"You reckon maybe Lessie Howell's got room for me?" she asked.

Ben's breath caught for a moment, and before he could answer, Mrs. Logan went on in that curiously humble voice, "You reckon if she has, she'd let me sleep in her house?"

"Of course she would, Mother. What a crazy question to ask!" Ben said huskily.

"Then I'm obliged to you all, but reckon if Lessie'll have me, I'd like best to go there," said Mrs. Logan, and for just a moment turned her face toward the smoking ruins of the home she had cherished for so many years. And then as Ben got into the car beside her, she locked her shaking hands tightly in her lap and turned her face forward.

Chapter 16

Lessie was alone on the front porch, looking across the road to where the old barn, a blaze of light, was filled with an appreciative audience, waiting for the performance to begin.

She was startled to hear the unmistakable sound of Ben's car in the lane, and her hands clenched tightly together. Seeing him now was a bitter, hurting sweetness, but she stood up as the car came slowly up the lane and Ben jumped out and came swiftly toward her.

"Lessie, I've got Mother with me," he said in a swift undertone. "The house burned to the ground this afternoon — "

"Oh, Ben, is she hurt?"

"Only shock and a very bad fright, but Doc Parmenter says she should be kept in bed two or three days. Will you — Lessie, I have no right to ask it — but will you let her stay here until I can make other arrangements?" His voice was low and ashamed.

"Oh, Ben, as if you had to ask that!" Her tone reproached him as she hurried to the car. "I'm terribly sorry about the house, Mrs. Logan, but it's so wonderful you were not hurt. Do come in."

"You're going to let me?" asked Mrs. Logan humbly.

"Oh, for goodness sake, what a silly question! I'd have been insulted if you'd gone anywhere else," protested Lessie, and swung open the door. She put out her hand to steady the old woman and then drew back, remembering Mrs. Logan's angry independence.

"Reckon I'll have to ask you to help me, Lessie," said Mrs. Logan. "Seems funny after all the years of doing for myself to have to ask folks' help, but I reckon I'm a mighty lucky woman to have somebody that will help me."

Ben lifted her out of the car and would have carried her to the steps, but unexpectedly, she made a faint struggle.

"Put me down on my feet, Ben. I can walk," she snapped, and Ben felt a relief almost as great as when Bill had come up from the plowed field carrying her.

He set her on her feet, and she clung to his arm. A fumbling hand went out to Lessie, who caught it in both her own, and between them they guided her up the steps and into the house.

"Smells good in here," said Mrs. Logan shyly, and then sniffed frankly. "I declare, it makes me remember I ain't had a bite to eat since noon. You reckon maybe you'd have a glass of milk and a little piece of cornbread, Lessie? Reckon being hungry's what makes me so all-fired weak."

Lessie laughed, and guided her toward the kitchen.

"You and Ben sit down and have some supper while I get a room ready for you," she urged.

"You sure we're not putting you out any? With all them play-actresses around, I was afraid maybe you wouldn't have room for a good-for-nothing old woman — "

"One more crack like that, and so help me, I'll paddle you," Ben threatened darkly. His eyes met Lessie's and pleaded with her and were overjoyed by the warmth and tenderness in her eyes.

"I got a lot to say to you, Lessie, but I reckon maybe I'd better wait till I get my strength back." Mrs. Logan eased herself into a chair at the table, while Lessie busied herself at the stove and Jim and Mary Sue, who had been doing the dishes, slid out of the room with a conspiratorial look.

Outside, well away from the house, they drew together in the shadow of a giant pine.

"What now?" breathed Mary Sue.

"Search me," answered Jim, as puzzled and uneasy as she. "I heard Ben say their house burned this afternoon. Do you suppose she expects to stay here? Permanently, I mean?"

"Well, I don't know of any place Ben can take her to — that she'd be willing to go to, I mean," worried Mary Sue. "Maybe if all of us are angel-good, and stay out of her way, she might be willing to let Ben marry Lessie."

"And then she'd live here forever! Boy, what a prospect!"

Jim was frankly appalled, and Mary Sue shivered.

"Well, it won't be so bad for you — you're going to be able to get away soon. But for Butch and Ellie and me — golly, Jim!"

"Yeah," Jim agreed, scowling. "And what about Lessie? It's going to be really rugged for her, having the old girl under foot every minute, sticking her nose into everything, giving orders — "

They turned and looked toward the kitchen, when brightly lighted windows showed them the scene as clearly as though it had been on the stage in the barn across the road. Lessie bringing laden plates from the stove, placing them in front of Ben and his mother; pouring coffee for Ben, milk for his mother and for herself, and sitting down with them. And they saw Ben put out his hand and cover Lessie's where it lay on the table and bring it to his lips.

"Golly," breathed Mary Sue, awed. "I've seen Charles Boyer do that in the movies, but imagine old Ben doing it!"

"It's because he loves her, stupe, and because he's grateful that she's taking his old harridan of a mother into the house," said Jim grimly.

"Well, he should be grateful! Boy, it's something I'd never do!"

Jim chuckled dryly. "You don't know what you'd do if you were in love, kid. Love makes you do some mighty funny things."

Mary Sue looked up at him sharply, but the shadow beneath the trees was so intense she could not see his expression. And Jim, feeling his face grow hot beneath the impact of his thought, was grateful for the shadow.

"How do you know so much about what being in love will do to you?" she demanded suspiciously.

"Oh," said Jim largely, "I read a book once."

"So did I," said Mary Sue, and started back to the house. "Lessie will want us to fix a room for the old battle-axe."

Jim caught her hand and drew her back to him.

"Listen, sprout, knock that chip off of your shoulder, you hear me? And never again let me hear you speak of an old woman in such a way! Do you hear?"

"Well, for Pete's sake, who are you to go giving me orders?" She was outraged and startled.

"I'm your brother, who's big enough to take a shingle to you if you don't behave yourself," said Jim, and his voice altered. "Look, Mary Sue. Remember how Mom used to say that if there was something you didn't want to do but that you couldn't get out of doing, the only smart thing was to be nice about it. So long as you've got to do it, you might as well change your thought about it, and do it with good will and it wouldn't be near so bad. You've heard her say it, haven't you?"

"Yes, of course. Lessie says it, too."

"So O.K. Mrs. Logan is here; it's likely she's going to stay for quite a spell. So we might as well make up our minds to it. She's our guest, and you can't be hateful to your guest. Mom said that, too, remember?"

"Sure I remember. But how are you going to love an old — oh, all right, an old lady as mean and selfish as she is?"

"Nobody asked you to love her. I'm just asking you to be respectful and pleasant. And I'm not asking you to do it for her sake, but for Lessie's. Things are going to be rough enough for Lessie without us getting our backs up and our claws out at the old — at Mrs. Logan. You can do it for Lessie, can't you?" Jim coaxed.

"Well, gosh, yes, of course. Come on!"

Mary Sue ran ahead of him onto the back porch and into the kitchen.

"Oh, there you are, Mary Sue. I wondered — " began Lessie.

"How do you do, Mrs. Logan? Hi, Ben!" Mary Sue's voice was sweet, so sweet that both Ben and Lessie shot her a sharp glance. Mary Sue went on, "Shall I fix a room for Mrs. Logan, Lessie?"

"Who's this?" demanded Mrs. Logan.

"My sister, Mary Sue, and my brother, Jim," answered Lessie as Jim followed Mary Sue into the kitchen.

"Howdy, children," said Mrs. Logan politely.

Mary Sue's eyes blazed at the "children" but Jim's hand was on her arm and he was saying pleasantly, "We're very sorry about your house, Mrs. Logan, but we're glad to have you with us. Mary Sue and I will get your room ready."

He guided Mary Sue out of the room, and Ben and Lessie, who had understood perfectly Mary Sue's indignation at being called a child, exchanged an amused glance.

"I declare, Lessie, you're a mighty fine cook," said Mrs. Logan, wiping her mouth elegantly after the last crumb of cake had disappeared from her plate. "Don't know when I've enjoyed a meal more."

"I'm sorry it had to be warmed over, and that supper was over before you came."

For a moment a tragic look touched the old woman's sightless eyes and she put her gnarled hands over her face.

"I was just starting to fix supper when it happened," she whispered desolately.

Lessie stood up swiftly and put her arms about the shaken shoulders.

"Try not to think about it, Mrs. Logan," she pleaded.

"You used to call me Aunt Nancy same as all the other young folks did," said Mrs. Logan humbly.

"Of course I did, Aunt Nancy," Lessie's voice made apology. "It's just that — well, I guess I forgot. Don't you think maybe now you'd better get some rest?"

"Maybe so, though I never did like to go to bed on a full stomach," said Mrs. Logan. She pushed back her chair and stood up, swaying slightly.

Ben was beside her instantly, his arm about her, and with Lessie guiding them, they went along the wide, old-fashioned hall that bisected the house and to an open door where Mary Sue and Jim were jerking covers straight on a big, puffy bed.

"Can you manage, Mother?" asked Ben, when Mary Sue and Jim had slid out of the room, as though fearful of any further contact with the old lady.

"Of course she can't, Ben, here in a strange place, but she's going to let me help her, aren't you, Aunt Nancy?" said Lessie gently.

"If you'll be so kind," said Mrs. Logan formally.

"Wait for me on the porch, Ben. I'll get her a night-gown," said Lessie under her breath.

When she had the old woman tucked into bed, she bent over and kissed her cheek lightly, compassion and tenderness in her gesture.

"You're mighty kind, Lessie, to a wicked, sinful old woman," Mrs. Logan said harshly.

"You're not wicked or sinful, Aunt Nancy; and even if you were, you're Ben's mother. We both love him, so why shouldn't we be kind to each other?"

"We'll talk about it later, Lessie. Seems

like I'm just about tuckered out." Mrs. Logan's voice spoke of her exhaustion, mental even more than physical.

"Of course, dear," said Lessie, and put out the light and went out to the porch where Ben was waiting for her.

Chapter 17

The morning rehearsal for next week's play was over, and the cast had scattered, some of them back to the village, for lunch at the new hotel and for whatever recreation the afternoon offered before the night's performance.

Teresa half lay, half sat in a big canvas beach chair behind the old barn-theatre, her favorite afternoon spot. She looked up with a slight frown as a young voice spoke behind her.

"May I speak to you a minute, Teresa?" asked Mary Sue hesitantly, her young face with its slightly tip-tilted nose and its small army of freckles grave and tense.

"Of course, Mary Sue. Come and sit down," invited Teresa, touched by the child's solemnity, even as she was puzzled by it.

"Teresa, would you let me go to New York with you and help me find a job?" The words tumbled out without Mary Sue's careful preparations having done her any good.

Teresa sat erect, staring at her.

"Certainly not, Mary Sue!" she said instantly.

Mary Sue recoiled as though Teresa had slapped her, and a dark crimson stain of humiliation spread over her face.

"Of course not. I was a fool to ask it. I'm sorry. It's just that I've got to get away from here somehow, and I thought maybe if you let Lessie think I was going with you —." Her miserable stammering faded to silence beneath the threat of tears as she started to get to her feet.

"Sit down, child." Teresa put out her hand and drew Mary Sue down once more. "Suppose you tell me all about it. Why do you have to get away from here? I thought you liked this heavenly place."

"Oh, I do, I love it. Only I've got to get away and somehow Butch and Ellie do, too. Jim's going into the Army, so that takes care of him. But — well, I don't know what to do with Butch and Ellie and me."

"Mary Sue, you're not making sense. Why do you all have to leave your home?" protested Teresa.

"So Mrs. Logan will let Ben marry Lessie."

"Oh, for the love of — Mary Sue, Ben's a man, quite grown up. If he is so weak-kneed he has to have his mother's consent before he marries Lessie, then Lessie is well rid of him!" snapped Teresa hotly.

"You don't understand, Teresa. His mother being blind and all, he couldn't marry Lessie and leave his mother to live alone. Well, now that their house has burned down, and she *had* to come here, where she swore she would never come — " Mary Sue gulped back a sob. "You see, Mrs. Logan said it wasn't fair for Ben to be burdened with 'a passel of young-'uns to raise.' So now if she still sticks to that, don't you see, we kids have got to get out from under foot, so she won't object any more. I could get married — only Bud's got to go in the Army the same time Jim does and — well, Mrs. Johnson likes me all right but she wouldn't, if I married Bud *now* — "

"You try marrying anybody, you infant, and I'll hold you while Lessie works you over — as I'm sure she would!" said Teresa firmly.

"But what are we going to do?" wailed Mary Sue.

"You're going to stop worrying, and leave everything to me," said Teresa firmly, and smiled warmly at her. "Ted — my husband — used to call me Mrs. Fixit! He said I always liked to think of myself as Helpful Harriet, but he was afraid there were times when people thought of me as Meddlesome

Mattie! Could be, I suppose, only my intentions are always of the very best! You know what good intentions are for, Mary Sue?"

Awed, hopeful in spite of herself, uneasy because of Teresa's sudden briskness, Mary Sue said, "No, I guess not."

"They are for paving stones in Hades," said Teresa, and there was a twinkle in her eyes that lifted Mary Sue's troubled young spirit. "I have the consolation of knowing mine make the very best quality of paving stones, though!"

She stood up with such an air of going to work that Mary Sue cried out in sudden alarm, "You're not going to tell Lessie about our talk?"

"I am not. I'm not even going to discuss this with Lessie," Teresa comforted her. "I'm after — well, bigger game."

Together they crossed the road, and as they came up the lane, met Angus starting across to his car, and Teresa called him.

"Wait for me, Andy? I've got an errand in town," she called.

"Sure, Teresa. What's up?" Angus was delighted at the change in her these past weeks. She had lost the haggard look, the strain and pallid sickliness that had struck straight at his heart. She had gained a few pounds, which she had badly needed, and she had a delicate, very becoming sun tan.

"I won't be long," she promised, and ran across the porch and into her own room.

Caro, seated by the window, going over the script for the next week's show, looked at her, startled as she began to strip off her slacks and shirt.

"Hi, where's the fire?" demanded Caro, and then looked guilty. "Not the most tactful remark one could make in the presence of the old girl across the hall — "

"I'm going to town for a while. Can I get you anything?" asked Teresa, stepping into a voluminous skirt of gaily printed cotton and whipping into a thin, cool blouse that tied in a bow in the back.

"Not unless you could find me a good memory somewhere that would make it possible for me to keep my lines for next week away from my lines for this week! And even if you could, I probably wouldn't be able to afford it."

Teresa laughed and ran out of the room, and Caro was delighted at her sudden youthful vigor.

Angus, waiting beside his convertible, felt his heart lift as she came hurrying toward him, pausing on her way to speak to a wide-eyed, troubled Mary Sue. She cupped the girl's chin in her palm, and grinned impishly at her.

"Chin up off the floor, Baby. You're wearing holes in the rug," she chided gaily. "You just leave everything to Auntie Teresa. We'll have the Logan gal eating out of your hand before you can say Jack Robinson."

"Jack Robinson!" said Mary Sue instantly, and laughed shakily.

"Was I long?" asked Teresa as she slid into the car and smiled at Angus, who was settling himself beside her.

"I wouldn't know. Waiting for you is never long — yet it is, too, in many ways. Waiting for you to be Teresa — as you used to be."

She smiled warmly at him, tenderness in her eyes.

"And the first thing you know, you'll turn your head and there she will be, standing right beside you," she promised, and before he could do more than give her a startled glance, she went busily on, "I wanted to talk to you — privately, darling. This seemed a wonderful chance. I wanted to talk to you about Lessie, Andy."

"Oh?" Angus was startled. "Something wrong with Lessie?"

Swiftly Teresa explained her scene with Mary Sue, and when she had finished, Angus was scowling.

"That's a rotten break for a couple of nice young people," he admitted. "Lessie's a doll. Ben's — well, Ben's a good guy after his own lights. He very definitely doesn't like me, so you can understand my not going overboard about him, though I will concede that he seems a decent sort."

"Well, to Lessie, he's the dream of her heart and we've got to fix things so that they can be married, and with the old girl's blessing and hearty co-operation," said Teresa firmly.

"That sounds like a large order, if you say that she is so opposed to Ben's taking on Lessie's responsibilities," admitted Angus.

"But don't you see, Andy? Or are the workings of the female mind too devious for your masculine instincts to follow? It's not the children that bother the old lady; it's Lessie."

"Any man alive would be lucky to get Lessie — "

"But don't you see? It's not just Lessie and the children; it's any girl who wants to marry her son! Oh, I grant you Mrs. Logan probably thinks it's the fact Ben would be taking on a lot of responsibilities, but if Lessie were an orphan, without a relative in the world, she would still find something to object to. Women, mothers especially, are the most ruthlessly selfish creatures ever born!"

"Hi, that's almost blasphemy!" protested Angus.

"It takes another woman to see it," Teresa admitted. "Mothers do *so* hate to let their youngsters loose from their apron strings. Especially a son."

Angus looked down at her, grinning.

"You're quite wrought up over all this, aren't you?" he asked, somewhat puzzled at her intense interest.

"Well, of course I am! Lessie adores that big lug! Oh, I shouldn't call him that, I know. It's Lessie who loves him, not me, and if she's satisfied with him, I'm tickled to pieces. Only she's got to have him, Andy, grim old witch of a mother or not. So what are we going to do about it?"

Angus raised his eyebrows above eyes that twinkled.

"Nothing!" he said firmly.

"Andy, you can't mean that!" She was outraged.

"*We* aren't going to do a thing. What business have we interfering? We're the rankest possible outsiders, darling. These mountain folks are clannish. They bitterly resent outsiders interfering — and there really isn't anything anybody can do. It's Ben's and Lessie's problem and they'll have to work it out."

Teresa said mutinously, "I'm *not* going to sit by with my hands folded and let that old girl wreck those two sweet kids!"

"Look, Honey, there's nothing you *can* do."

"I bet I'll think of something! You just wait!" Teresa's eyes were dark and her jaw was set at a defiant angle that Angus had learned long ago to respect.

He sighed and shook his head, but there was a twinkle in his eyes.

"I learned a long time ago that when you get that look on your face, whoever you're fighting had better take to the storm cellars," he admitted.

She looked at him swiftly, a troubled look in her eyes.

"You mean I'm ruthless?" she asked uneasily.

"Let's say determined!" Angus was speaking lightly, his attention on the road ahead where traffic was thickening as they approached the village.

She was silent for a moment, and then she said huskily, "Andy, darling, when are you going to marry me?"

Beneath his startled grip on the wheel, the car lurched dangerously, and when he had it under control, he looked down at her, a savage momentary anger in his eyes.

"That wasn't funny, Teresa," he warned her.

"It wasn't meant to be, darling."

They were almost within sight of the village, but a narrow, winding road little more than a trail turned off at right angles, and Angus maneuvered the car into it, slammed on the brakes and turned to her. His face was white beneath its summer tan and his eyes were blazing.

"Just what was it meant to be, then?" he demanded.

"Well, it's been a wonderful summer, Andy darling. And I — well, I sort of got the impression that you liked me more than a little, but I guess I was wrong. Maybe if I'd kept my mouth shut — "

His hands were on her shoulders, turning her sharply around to face him. And when she could not meet his eyes, but closed her own, he gave her a small, hard shake.

"Look at me, Teresa," he ordered.

When at last she did, his eyes probed hers for a long, shaken moment, but still he did not draw her into his arms. He could only look down at her, afraid to believe the shining wonder in her eyes.

"Teresa!" he said at last, his voice so low and shaken it was scarcely more than a whisper. "Teresa, my darling, my darling!"

A tremulous smile curved her soft mouth, and she blinked hard against the mist of tears in her eyes.

"Does that mean, Andy darling, that maybe you will?" she stammered, like a young girl abashed and awed by the wonder of first love.

"Teresa — oh, Teresa, are you sure?" His voice was still low and shaken. "I lost you once to Ted; I couldn't endure losing you again if you were being just fooled by a sort of summer madness."

"You know me better than that, darling! Ted *was* my first love; I'll never forget him. You wouldn't want me to. He'll always be my red roses in December. But Ted's gone, darling, and I've been so terribly lonely. It's — oh, Andy, it's wonderful to be alive again, to come out of the darkness and into the sunlight. Darling, I love you so much! It's a different love, but it's just as wonderful. We have so much in common; we're such wonderful companions. You're so sweet and dear. I love being with you. Oh, Andy, couldn't we make a good life together now?"

There were no words to answer that. Words were not needed; Angus held her close and hard against him, and their kiss was deep with a yearning tenderness that would live forever between them.

Chapter 18

Mrs. Logan sat in a deep old-fashioned rocker on the front porch in the late afternoon, her sightless face turned toward the mountains she knew were there but that she had not seen for so many years and that she would never see again. But they were printed so clearly on her heart she would always hold the picture dear.

Across the road she could hear the small sounds of activity as the theatre was prepared for its evening performance. But above and beyond those sounds, she heard those that were of her own experience. This is the saddest, most poignant time of the day even to those whose eyes see clearly — the homecoming hour. To women like herself, with her home gone, herself a stranger in a strange place, the hour held only bitter sadness.

She heard Ben's car, and then he came up on the porch and crossed to her, and bent to kiss her cheek. She put her hand and held his face to hers for a moment; and then, abashed by the unaccustomed caress, for she was not a demonstrative woman, she drew away from him.

"Are you feeling all right, Mother?" asked Ben gently.

"Why wouldn't I be? Bone-lazy, setting here like an old Dominecker hen on a nestful of eggs, letting folks wait on me hand and foot!" Her voice held only a trace of its former harshness, and then she said quickly, "Not but what Lessie and the young-'uns don't take mighty good care of me. Though why they'd bother, as mean and ornery as I've been, I don't know."

"They are fond of you, Mother." The lie stuck in Ben's throat painfully.

"Ha!" Mrs. Logan's derisive snort dismissed the word. "Why should they be? Except because they're kinder than anybody's got a right to expect other folks to be. That's a right fine passel of young-'uns Lessie's got, Ben. I sure hate it that Jim's got to go off to war. Seems like I can't remember when fine young boys like him haven't had to go into the service, before they're dry behind the ears. Butch is the quiet one," she mused. "Polite as all get-out, but I don't hear him around much. What's the matter with him?"

"Oh, he likes hunting and fishing and getting off to himself to tramp the mountains," answered Ben.

"Sounds a mite like you when you was his age," commented his mother. "I just hope he's the man you are, son."

"He'll be a much better one, Mother. He's going to be a doctor, he says."

Mrs. Logan raised her face swiftly.

"That'll take a sight o' money. Learning doctoring's a long, hard road and costs a lot for schooling," she protested.

Ben's jaw tightened slightly.

"Lessie started a savings account for him when the show people moved in on her," he said tautly. "And Mr. MacDonnell has already told her the season was so successful that he wants the barn again next year. Butch will have his training, don't worry about that."

Mrs. Logan's shoulders stiffened slightly.

"I'm not worrying — why should I? It's none of my business," she flashed at him.

Ben straightened and his face was grim.

"If you'll excuse me, Mother, I'll go clean up for supper," he told her, and she heard his firm, measured tread going across the porch and up the stairs.

She sat on in the gathering dusk until Ellie's piping voice aroused her.

"Supper's ready, Aunt Nancy. You take my hand and let me help you, won't you?" she invited, and a small, plump hand slid into the old woman's work-scarred, clawlike grip.

Lessie watched anxiously as Ellie guided the old woman along the hall, and to her chair at the foot of the table, while Butch, Mary Sue and Jim waited at their own places. No one spoke as Ellie guided Mrs. Logan to her chair and into it, just as Ben came into the room, his hair sleek and wet, showing the comb-marks, the open collar of his fresh shirt revealing the muscular column of his sun-tanned neck.

"We're having chicken and dumplings, Aunt Nancy," announced Lessie eagerly. "I do hope the dumplings are light enough. I never have been able to make them as good as Mother did. Maybe you can tell me what I do that's wrong."

"Dumplings take a sight of practice, Lessie. Reckon your Maw put in a many a year learning to get 'em light and flaky like, same as me," said Mrs. Logan, heavily polite, still smarting from the necessity of having to be led around by the hand.

Ben, sensing this, launched into an amusing story of the day, and the others chimed in, and supper passed without further comment from Mrs. Logan.

Lessie, covertly watching her, saw with relief that Mrs. Logan's appetite had im-

Jane winced. "Does it show that much?" She asked pitifully.

"I'm afraid so," admitted Caro with merciful brutality. "It's like a three alarm fire, difficult to conceal. Too bad."

"But isn't there some way — " Jane began, and then her voice broke. When she spoke again there was an edge of anger in her voice. "And don't tell me he's too old for me! That's what *he* says, and it isn't true! He's just exactly right! No one will ever be so right for me again!"

"You poor kid!" said Caro quietly. "Hurts like blazes, doesn't it?"

Jane, startled momentarily out of her self-absorption, looked swiftly at Caro.

"You, too?" she stammered.

"Me, too," said Caro heavily. "I was about your age, homely, though, a comedienne who yearned to be a big dramatic star. He was a matinee-idol type. I didn't have a ghost of a chance from the very first. But I can still remember how it hurt when he married somebody else; and then a divorce and somebody else, and so on, until he had had five wives and died alone. Every time he divorced a wife, my heart stood up on its hind legs and yipped like an excited puppy — the fool a human heart can be! Because I was so sure I was the woman who could have made him happy."

She jerked herself out of her memories and said sharply, "See here, you! What do you mean sending me wallowing into memories I thought I'd discarded years ago? Memories can be pure, unadulterated Hades, if you let 'em. Me, I've always followed the philosophy of never looking back, and not too far ahead! Good night!"

She stalked away, leaving Jane to stare after her, wide-eyed and deeply disturbed.

She was still standing there alone when Mason came over to her and said quietly, "If you're ready I'll drive you home."

She nodded, without a word, and led the way out of the barn.

In the car, she sat for a moment looking out into the moon-drenched meadow, and Mason looked down at her before he started the car.

"Swell about Andy and Teresa, isn't it? He's been in love with her for a long time; I think everybody that knew them both has known that for years," he said cautiously.

"That's the terrible thing about being hopelessly in love. Everybody seems to know about it except the one that really matters, the one you love," said Jane softly, without looking at him. "Caro just told me about being in love with a man all these years — and watching him marry five different women, and divorce them all while she was still waiting, her heart in her hands, wanting so terribly to give it to him, only he didn't seem to know it was there. That's a terrible waste, isn't it?"

"Jane," said Mason very low, and his voice was rough and shaken with tenderness. "Jane, my dearest dear, I'm not much of a bargain, and I'm much too old for you and I may not even be able to support you, take decent care of you. But I'm here, and if you really think you want me I'd be very pleased indeed if you'd marry me."

Jane sat very still, afraid to believe that she had really heard him. And then very carefully, as if afraid her smallest movement might wreck the moment and destroy the words she had heard, turned her head and looked at him.

"You wouldn't mind?" she whispered, her tone touched with awe and wonder, with a humility that was achingly sweet to him, yet that somehow hurt him, too.

There was only one possible answer to that. His arms drew her close to him, and his voice was little more than a breath of sound when he spoke her name; but his mouth on hers was gentle, and compelling in its urgent tenderness.

Chapter 19

Mrs. Logan sat on the porch, her hands folded in unaccustomed idleness. From the big cool back porch she could hear the voices of the children as they helped Lessie, and the knowledge that there were household tasks and garden duties that she would never be able to do again made her set her teeth so hard in her lower lip that the blood almost came.

She welcomed the light footstep that came across the porch, and then a soft, cool mass of fragrance was laid in her arms, and her wondering old hands, bent and work-scarred, touched the blossoms as though she touched a well-loved baby's velvet cheek.

"Roses!" she whispered incredulously. "Roses right here late in August, and smelling so grand! I bet they're red roses. But I never saw such stems. Why, they must be a yard long!"

Teresa laughed softly. "They are red roses, and they're from a florist in Atlanta. I had one of the boys bring them up for you. A very wise and wonderful man once said, 'God gave us memories, so we can have red roses in December.' It's only August, but too late for roses up here — this kind of roses, anyway!"

"Now that was mighty kind and thoughtful of you, Miss Carr," said Mrs. Logan.

Teresa sat down beside her and put her hand on the bony old knee beneath the long, crisp calico skirts.

"The roses are really a bribe, Mrs. Logan," she said gently.

Puzzled, Mrs. Logan turned her face.

"A bribe?" she repeated, astonished.

"There's something I want you to do for me, Mrs. Logan," said Teresa, choosing her words with painstaking care.

"Now, what could an old blind woman like me do for you, Miss Carr?" Mrs. Logan demanded. "You're just funnin' with me."

"Mrs. Logan, I've grown very fond of Lessie and the children," said Teresa quietly.

"Reckon that wasn't hard to do. Seems like they're a right nice crowd of young-'uns. Lessie, too, is a fine girl."

"Of course she is, Mrs. Logan," said Teresa eagerly. "I'm especially fond of Ellie, and I want to adopt her."

For an instant Mrs. Logan went rigid, her hands gripping the roses until the thorns bit into her flesh.

"Adopt Ellie?" she gasped incredulously. "Take her away with you next week?"

"Yes," said Teresa, and rushed on, "You may have heard that Mr. MacDonnell and I are going to be married. We can do so much for Ellie, and we'd adore to have her. And I have thought, too, that we can easily take Mary Sue, too, and provide for her future. Jim is going into the Army, and that will leave only Butch to be cared for."

Mrs. Logan's voice was outraged.

"You must be out of your mind, Miss Carr," she blazed. "Why, Lessie'd run you off the place if she thought you were even thinking — you ain't talked to Lessie about this, have you?"

"Well, no," Teresa admitted. "I wanted to talk to you first and get you on my side."

"Well, you're sure wastin' your breath! Why, I never heard of anything so awful in my life!" blazed Mrs. Logan, and thrust the roses from her. "Her that's give almost her whole life to them young-'uns — "

"But don't you think that now Lessie has a right to a life for herself?" Teresa cut in quietly.

Mrs. Logan jerked as though she had been slapped.

"And just what do you mean by that, ma'am?" she asked hotly.

"Well, after all, Lessie and your son are very much in love," Teresa pointed out gently. "They have been practically all their lives, as I understand it. And your son shouldn't be expected to burden himself with a whole houseful of somebody else's children."

Mrs. Logan snorted with fury.

"What business have you got telling my son what he should do? He's a grown man, and I reckon he'd always meet his responsibilities same as the men in his family have always done!"

Teresa kept her voice quiet, but her eyes were warm and dancing.

"I'm sorry if I've spoken out of turn, Mrs. Logan, but I understood that you objected to your son's marriage to Lessie."

"That's none of your business, ma'am!" There was concentrated venom in Mrs. Logan's voice. "We don't need flat-landers like you and the rest of them show folks to come here and tell us what we got to do. You just get your things together soon as you can and git out of here! And don't you say a word to Lessie about adopting Ellie. The very idea!"

"I'm afraid I can't promise that, Mrs. Logan," said Teresa.

"Well, you'd better! If Ben ever heard of

this — he don't like you show folks much anyway — this'd just about finish him with all of you!" There were spots of color in Mrs. Logan's brown face.

"Mrs. Logan, Mary Sue came to me herself the day after your place burned and told me that you wouldn't allow Ben to marry Lessie because of the children, and asked me to take her to New York with me and help her find work." Teresa came out with what she knew would be a brutal blow, but she could think of no way to soften the truth; and Mrs. Logan must have the truth, all of it.

"Mary Sue told you that?" Mrs. Logan's voice was little more than a stricken whisper. "She wants to get away because I'm here?"

"She wants to leave Lessie free to marry Ben. And why not? They have a right to a normal, happy life," began Teresa.

"'Well, they don't have to get rid of the young-'uns for that! They can get rid of *me* — "

Teresa was deeply touched by the heartbreak in the old woman's voice, and quickly she covered the shaking old hands with her own that were warm and soft and well-kept.

"They don't want to get rid of you, Mrs. Logan. Why should they? You're Ben's mother and he loves you, and because she loves Ben, Lessie would love you, too, if you'd let her," she said gently.

"If I'd let her?" Mrs. Logan whispered uncomprehendingly.

"I don't want to hurt you, Mrs. Logan, but I feel you're a woman big enough and honest enough to be willing to face the truth," said Teresa, wishing for a moment she had never started this, yet still convinced it had had to be done. "You came here with a chip on your shoulder; you're sorry for yourself."

"That's a lie!"

"Is it?" Teresa probed relentlessly. "You're feeling abused and mistreated because your house burned. That's bad, I know. But can't you see how worried Ben has always been, leaving you there alone all day while he was off at work? He's dreaded and feared that this might happen. Now that it's over, and you can no longer insist on your precious independence, can't you see that it has, in many ways, taken a load off his mind and his heart?"

Mrs. Logan sat huddled, seeming suddenly shrunken, her face turned away from Teresa, who drew a deep breath, hating herself yet still feeling that she must go on.

"I've always tried to feel, Mrs. Logan, that bad things come to us for some good purpose," she said gently. "Oh, I know it's awfully hard many times to understand why they should happen. When my husband died, I wanted just to go and crawl in a hole and feel sorry for myself. I did, too, for a long time. And then — well, you're not interested in the means by which I finally, with darling Andy's help and that of my friends, pulled myself out of it and saw that life was good. Oh, I still don't understand the purpose back of Ted's death. Some day, maybe, I will, just as some day you will understand your house being burned — and your life being saved. Don't you see, Mrs. Logan? Instead of resenting it, of grieving, and all the rest, you should be grateful for Ben, and for Lessie and for grandchildren to enjoy! Because the children are such darlings!"

"I don't need you to tell me that!" Mrs. Logan was still defiant but there was less fire in her voice.

Teresa stood up. "I'm sorry if I've hurt you, Mrs. Logan, but I felt it was something that had to be said. It had to come from an outsider, for both Ben and Lessie love you too much to be willing to hurt you, even when it is for your own good."

"My own good!"

"It is, Mrs. Logan, believe me. Why, you're strong and healthy. You've got many more years of happy, useful life."

"Useful? How can an old blind bat like me be useful to anybody?" It was more of a wail than an exclamation.

"By using the faculties that have made it possible for you to live alone and look after your house. You're in a strange place now, but how long would it take you to familiarize yourself with it, if you'd only try!"

"Being led around by the hand by one of the young-'uns?" Mrs. Logan's voice was aching and bitter.

"Why not? What's shameful about that? Be grateful there are children who are willing and anxious to lead you around. Think of the thousands of blind people who have to depend on Seeing Eye dogs to lead them around, and who manage to lead busy happy lives in spite of that."

Mrs. Logan stiffened beneath the sting in Teresa's voice, but she had her features well under control now.

"I'm obliged to you, Miss Carr, for telling me the truth," she said painfully. "I reckon now I'd like to just sit here and think a spell."

"Of course, Mrs. Logan," said Teresa, and added softly, "Don't hate me too much."

"I don't waste time hatin' folks," snapped Mrs. Logan. And then as Teresa turned away, she added diffidently, "Miss Carr, would you please, ma'am, put my roses in water so they'll live a long time?"

"Oh, of course, Mrs. Logan, I'd love to," Teresa caught up the roses and held them gently, looking down at the woman's tired old face. "Will you ever forgive me, Mrs. Logan?"

"Reckon folks has a right to speak the truth — and shame the devil," said Mrs. Logan grimly. "Reckon that's what I've been — a she-devil."

"You don't have to be, Mrs. Logan," Teresa persisted, and now her tone was gentle.

"Reckon it's not easy to teach an' old dog new tricks," Mrs. Logan told her brusquely, and added impulsively, "That's unless the old dog wants to learn."

Teresa hesitated a moment, and then, because Mrs. Logan had turned her face away, Teresa went lightly across the porch and into the house.

For a long time after Teresa had gone, Mrs. Logan sat alone, her hands tightly folded in her lap.

Chapter 20

Mary Sue came into the kitchen the next morning, her eyes wide.

"Lessie, have we got a good stout walking stick?" she demanded.

Startled, Lessie looked up.

"A walking stick, Mary Sue? What do you want with a walking stick?"

"I don't," Mary Sue assured her dramatically. "It's Aunt Nancy."

"But what in the world — "

"She says she's tired of settin' like an old hen on a nest, and she wants to learn how to get around the place by herself, like she did at home. And she thinks a cane would steady her and she could use it to poke out in front of her and see she doesn't stumble or fall down."

For a moment the two sisters stared at each other.

"Mary Sue, why do you think she wants to get accustomed to this place? Ben told her last night he had found a house for them, and as soon as it had been furnished, they would move. She seemed pleased and excited," Lessie pointed out uneasily. "But if she gets accustomed to it here, then she'll have to start all over again somewhere else."

Mary Sue hesitated a moment and then she asked fearfully, "Lessie, do you think maybe she's planning to stay here and let you and Ben get married?"

Lessie caught her breath beneath the impact of that thought, and then she saw Mary Sue's troubled eyes and asked very softly, "Would you and the others mind so much, darling, if she did want to stay on?"

"'Well, gosh, I don't know!" Mary Sue admitted in a burst of youthful frankness. "I'm scared stiff of her most of the time, but she's — well, so sort of pitiful. I keep looking at her and thinking, Well, gollies, pal, one of these days you'll be old and maybe blind or crippled and in the way; don't you hope that when you are there'll be somebody young and strong around that will give you a break? Gollies, Lessie, it must be just awful to be old and helpless and dependent on somebody's kindness so you don't have to just sit like a bump on a log like she does, when we're all busy and don't have time to worry about her."

"Thanks, honey," said Lessie, and her eyes were warm and wet. "I needed that little lecture. I'll try to profit by it!"

Mary Sue's eyes were wide with astonishment.

"Oh, shucks, who'd try to lecture you, Lessie? Why, you're like the gang at school says. You're the most, to say the least!"

"Well, that's a compliment I really appreciate," Lessie laughed. "Now, let's see if we can find one of Grandsir's old canes. I seem to remember there's one up in the attic."

Lessie rummaged in a corner of the attic and came up with a stout, thick no-nonsense-about-it cane with a curved handle and held it up in triumph.

"Think she'll like this, Mary Sue?" she asked. "There's a fancy one somewhere; Grandsir called it his Sunday-go-to-meeting cane, but it's not as stout and dependable as this one."

Mary Sue accepted it. "She'll be tickled bright pink — I hope," she answered, and started down the stairs.

Lessie waited in the big, cool old hall while Mary Sue went out to where Mrs. Logan sat in the shady front porch.

"Lessie found this one, Aunt Nancy," Lessie heard Mary Sue say. "It was Grandsir's, and I think he'd be glad for you to have it."

"Well, now, I'm right proud of it, Mary Sue." Lessie heard a new eagerness in Mrs.

Logan's voice. "Now, if you'll just guide me along the porch, so's I can count the steps a few times, reckon I'll be fine. Now don't you move nothing out of my way; you just tell me where it is so I can walk around it. I don't aim to have nobody upsetting their arrangements just on my account. Soon's I get used to things, I'll be able to look after myself and not weary you young-'uns."

"You don't weary us, Aunt Nancy," Mary Sue assured her earnestly. "We love having you here."

Mrs. Logan said gently, "Reckon that's one of the nicest things a body in my place could hear, Mary Sue. I'm obliged to you."

Lessie slipped back to the kitchen and went on making apple pies for lunch, puzzled and trying to understand what Mrs. Logan had in mind. But she had by no means reached a solution when Caro appeared at the door.

"Hi, there," she greeted Lessie affectionately. "Would I be the world's perfect nuisance if I asked to have lunch with you and the family? Or are you so glad next week is the end of the season and we're going to be out from underfoot you'd rather not bother?"

"Don't talk foolishment," Lessie laughed. "I'm going to miss you all like the dickens."

Caro eyed her with swift, affectionate sympathy.

"No hint of the old gal weakening?" she asked softly, nodding toward the porch where they could hear Mary Sue and Mrs. Logan, and the faint tapping of the stout cane.

"I don't know," admitted Lessie quietly. "She asked for a walking cane, and wanted Mary Sue to help her get accustomed to walking by guiding herself with the cane. I can't understand. Ben has found a house for them, and they will move into it as soon as Ben can get it furnished."

"You don't think maybe that she's planning on staying on here, with her objection to Ben's marriage wiped out? Or is that too much to hope for, do you think?" asked Caro softly.

"I don't know what to think, and I don't know what I dare to hope for," admitted Lessie. "It's — well, we'll just have to wait and see."

Caro said thoughtfully, "People reverence motherhood and mother love and so they should, so they should. But there are mothers who seem to want to devour their children, like the black widow spider her mate. Like Jane's mother, who wants Jane to be an actress and doesn't give a tinker's damn what Jane wants; and like Mrs. Logan who will not let go of her son — Sorry, Lessie. But that's the way it looks to me. Here, let me help you with that."

They worked together companionably for a while, and then Lessie called to the others that lunch was ready and they came trooping in. All save Mary Sue and Mrs. Logan.

There was the tapping of the cane, and then Mrs. Logan came into the kitchen, Mary Sue a few steps behind her, but not touching or guiding her.

"There! Now I can walk the full length of the porch and down the hall to the kitchen, and nobody had to guide me! Mary Sue helped me, but I won't be needing her much," she boasted eagerly. "I can find my chair, too."

With the stick probing ahead of her, she moved cautious step by step until she had reached the chair, gripped it and seated herself, lifting her beaming face from one to the other, so overjoyed at her momentary success that all felt the sting of tears.

"Don't nobody tell Ben, though," she pleaded as they settled about the table. "I want to surprise him. I want to go down the front steps and along the walk to his car, all by myself, with just my cane, to greet him. I bet he'll be some surprised."

"I bet he will, too," said Caro, and patted

Mrs. Logan's hand. "You're quite a woman, Mrs. Logan. I'm proud to know you."

Mrs. Logan stiffened and tilted her head, listening.

"Who are you? It's not Miss Carr, I know."

"I'm Teresa's friend, Caro Somers."

"One of the show people?"

"Yes. Do you mind?"

"Why should I mind? Lessie's put up with you all summer; none of my business, of course. If it was what she wanted to do, reckon it was her affair, not mine." Mrs. Logan spoke grumpily, and then looked almost guilty. "I guess I forgot I was in Lessie's house, not my own; it's not my business who Lessie has in her house. I'm right glad to meet you, Miss Somers."

Caro looked at Lessie, shrugged and spread her hands in a little gesture that acknowledged her defeat. And Lessie, lowering her eyes to her plate, set her teeth hard in her lower lip. Any brief hope she may have had that Mrs. Logan had changed in any respect died before it could flower. For some purpose of her own, Mrs. Logan wished to familiarize herself with the Howell place, but it was obvious she had no intention of remaining here any longer than was necessary. The leopard had not changed its spots, she reminded herself drearily. Mrs. Logan was as opposed to staying here, to permitting Ben to marry Lessie, as she had always been, and Lessie's heart drooped the wings it had so briefly dared to wear.

Chapter 21

Ben turned the car into the lane, glancing across at the old barn, shuttered and closed for the winter, its gaily clothed, chattering crowd gone. There was something very lonely about it now, with the great doors boarded up and the windows shuttered, but Ben was glad that the whole summer crowd was gone. It had seemed to him a very long summer, and he would be glad to get settled back in a place of his own, with his mother. No, he was lying, he told himself grimly. He would not be glad to have a place of his own with his mother; what he wanted was Lessie and her family to love and to help her bring up. Not that she needed help, he had to admit; she had done a fine job.

He brought the car to its accustomed parking place and shut off the motor. And then, startled, incredulous, he looked at the porch and saw his mother, alone, walking across the porch with swift, sure steps and along the walk, as she had come to meet him countless times when they had lived in the old house.

"That you, Ben?" Her voice was alight with loving laughter as he moved swiftly to meet her.

"Why, Mother, you're walking all by yourself! Aren't you afraid you'll stumble?"

"I got Grandsir's stick to help me," she boasted. "And this afternoon, Ellie and me weeded Lessie's flower bed and divided the peony clumps."

"Why, that's wonderful!"

"Lessie's got so much to do in the house, canning and preserving and all. I always took care of my flowers and she's got some mighty pretty ones. I knew I couldn't help her in the kitchen, so I told her I'd weed and mulch the flowers and get 'em all bedded down for winter, same as I always did at home."

Ben put his arm about her and held her close for a moment.

"Ben, you reckon there's any of that spiderwort, the blue and white kind, and any of them foxgloves left over home? Or did the fire get my flowers, too?" she asked softly.

"How'd you like to drive over there tomorrow morning and see?" suggested Ben.

"Have you got the time?" she asked eagerly.

"I'll take the time. I haven't been over since the fire, except that one time to be sure the furnishings and all were gone. But I didn't notice about the flowers."

"Then we'll go tomorrow. I reckon Lessie'd be right proud to have some foxgloves; they're mighty sightly, and she ain't got a one. Maybe there's some other things I could bring her, too," she said happily, and turned toward the house. "Time you get washed up, supper will be on the table."

Ben walked beside her back to the house, but she would not allow him to touch her, prideful of the ease with which she walked, the sureness with which she mounted the steps and crossed the porch to the hall.

"I'll go on down to the kitchen and see is there anything I can do to help Lessie, while you get cleaned up, son," she told him happily.

When he came back to the kitchen, the family had gathered about the table, and Ellie was leaning against Mrs. Logan's shoulder, in the middle of some childish talk to which his mother was listening with every evidence of absorbed attention.

Ben went to the stove, where Lessie lifted her face to greet him. As he kissed her, he asked softly, "How long has this been going on?"

"For more than a week," Lessie answered. "It's amazing how fast she has learned to get about; and she is wonderful with the garden. She wouldn't let us tell you. She wanted to surprise you."

"That she did, that she did!" agreed Ben, and took the big stoneware platter from her and placed it on the table.

They gathered about the table in the yellow lamp-light, and plates were served and there was silence while the keen edge was taken from everybody's hunger. And then Mrs. Logan pushed her plate aside, and faced Lessie across the table from her.

"Lessie, I ain't very good at saying I'm sorry. I reckon I'm just a ornery old woman that's always wanted her own way out of life and, when she couldn't get it, just started kicking and scratching and bawling like a spoiled two year-old brat that needs a good hard paddling. But I'm telling you now, Lessie; you and the young-'uns and Ben. I'm real ashamed of the way I've been acting. Feeling sorry for myself. Why, my Paw always said folks that went around feeling sorry for themselves was right sorry folks to begin with. And I reckon he was right."

"Now, you stop low-rating yourself, Aunt Nancy," protested Lessie quite sincerely. "You had a right to feel sorry for yourself, losing your home and all — "

"I didn't lose my home, Lessie. All I lost

was my house. Ben is my home; wherever Ben is, there is my home," Mrs. Logan cut in, her voice shaken slightly. "And the Lord has been mighty good to me, to give me Ben — and maybe, if you-all will let me stay here, a family, too. A mighty fine family. Maybe you'd let me be Gran'ma! I lost me a house, but I found me a mighty fine family, if they'll have me."

"Why, Aunt Nancy, we'd love having you, wouldn't we, children?" cried Lessie.

"Well, sure, Aunt Nancy — " That was Jim.

"Of course — " beamed Mary Sue.

"Sure will." Butch's smile made up for his abashed voice.

"A grandmother!" breathed Ellie, wide-eyed, entranced. "Think o' me having a gran'ma like the other kids at school! I've always *wanted* a gran'ma, and I didn't think I'd ever have one."

"You come to Granny, Honey." Mrs. Logan caught the child close in her arms and held her, and for a moment no one could speak above lumps in their throats.

It was Mrs. Logan who broke the emotional tension of the moment, and there were tears on her cheeks when she turned her face to Lessie and to Ben.

"I'm so sorry and ashamed for the things

I said to you that day you come to see me, Lessie," she pleaded. "Reckon maybe the house getting burned up was punishment on me for trying to keep you and Ben apart. Me, that's lived my life, trying to live Ben's for him — to deny him the right of any man to his own life. Reckon if Ben hadn't been the fine boy he is, he'd have walked out on me and left me there and come on over here and married you, Lessie. It would have served me right — "

"You knew I wouldn't do that, Mother!"

She reached out her hand, and Ben caught it in both his own.

"No," she said softly. "I know you ain't the kind that could do a thing like that, even if it was what I deserved. But now — if you can put up with me, Lessie, I'd like it a heap if you'd marry my boy and let us all live here together. Maybe I could be a little help; I'll tote my share and try not to be a burden."

"Aunt Nancy, don't talk like that." Lessie was around the table, her arms about the old woman, who clung to her suddenly and hid her sightless face against Lessie's shoulder. "Oh, if only you could be happy here, Aunt Nancy, we'd all be so glad! So very glad!"

Mrs. Logan held one of Lessie's hands,

and one of Ben's, and she turned from one to the other as though she could see them with her physical eyes rather than the eyes of her heart.

"I mind something you said that last time you come to see me, Lessie, when I was being purely mean and spiteful. You said me and you both loved Ben and we wanted him to be happy; and we was the two women he loved best in the world, so the only way we could hurt him was by not getting along good together. Well, Lessie, I'm sure going to do my share, and you'll do more than yours, like you've always done. Looks to me like everything ought to work out right nice!"

"Right nice?" Ben repeated, and stood up swiftly and caught Lessie close, his eyes adoring her. "Right perfect! Oh, Mother — Lessie — kids — "

"Hooray for us!" said Jim softly, and chuckled. "Wouldn't you know I'd be checking out just about the time everything worked out for everybody?"

Mrs. Logan turned anxiously to him.

"Jim, if you don't want to go in the army, maybe we could do something about it," she suggested eagerly.

Jim looked sharply at her, frowning.

"Like what, for instance?" he asked curiously.

"Well, I don't know exactly," Mrs. Logan admitted. "But there *has* been folks up here that's kept their boys home, claiming they was needed on the farm; widowed mothers and all — "

"Thanks, that's swell, Mrs. Logan — I mean Gran'-ma," said Jim, chuckling. "But I can't think of any place where I'm going to be needed less than right here. And besides, I want to go! I've been looking forward to it, only I hated leaving Lessie without a man around the house. Now that she's got Ben, and you, too, Gran'ma, well, I'm off in a cloud of dust!"

They smiled at him, anxiety in Lessie's eyes, and Jim went on after a moment, "There's just one thing I want you all to promise me."

"What's that, son?" asked Mrs. Logan anxiously.

"And that is that you'll all be right here, together, just like this, when I come back!" said Jim.

"It's a promise," they all chorused.

Ben's arms tightened about Lessie and drew her out of the lamplit kitchen and to the old back porch, where for a long and precious moment they could be alone to savor the perfection of this moment they had scarcely dared to hope for, yet toward which their hearts had been strained since they first met.

"Oh, Ben!" she whispered at last, her heart too full for the words that need not be said.

"I know, my darling, my dearest — I know," said Ben huskily.

And then there were no further words between them.

The employees of THORNDIKE PRESS hope you have enjoyed this Large Print book. All our Large Print books are designed for easy reading — and they're made to last.

Other Thorndike Large Print books are available at your library, through selected bookstores, or directly from us. Suggestions for books you would like to see in Large Print are always welcome.

For more information about current and upcoming titles, please call or mail your name and address to:

THORNDIKE PRESS
PO Box 159
Thorndike, Maine 04986
800/223-6121
207/948-2962